THE ZOO at the EDGE OF THE WORLD

by

ERIC KAHN GALE

Illustrations by Sam Nielson

BALZER + BRAY
An Imprint of HarperCollins Publishers

Balzer + Bray is an imprint of HarperCollins Publishers.

The Zoo at the Edge of the World
Text copyright © 2014 by Eric Kahn Gale
Illustrations copyright © 2014 by Sam Nielson
Map art copyright © 2014 by Mike Schley

www.harpercollinschildrens.com

Library of Congress Cataloging-in-Publication Data
Gale, Eric Kahn, date
  The Zoo at the Edge of the World / by Eric Kahn Gale ; illustrations by Sam Nielson.
— First edition.
    pages cm
  Summary: "Marlin, a stutterer, can talk smoothly and freely with the jungle animals that
populate his father's zoo in South America—until a mysterious man-eating black jaguar
that his father catches and brings back home talks back"— Provided by publisher.
  ISBN 978-0-06-212517-0 (pbk.)
  [1. Human-animal communication—Fiction. 2. Jungle animals—Fiction. 3. Zoos—
Fiction. 4. Stuttering—Fiction.] I. Nielson, Sam, illustrator. II. Title.
PZ7.G13134Zo 2014   2014002144
[Fic]—dc23   CIP
                                                                           AC

Typography by Erin Fitzsimmons
15 16 17 18 19 CG/OPM 10 9 8 7 6 5 4 3 2 1
❖
First paperback edition, 2015

The
ZOO
at the
EDGE
of the
WORLD

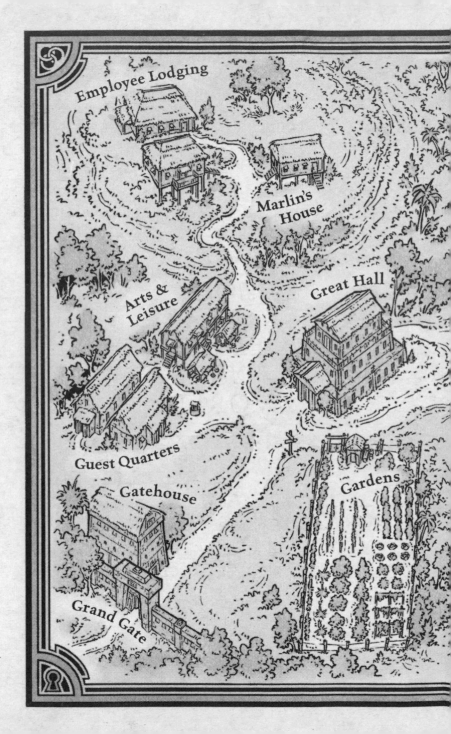

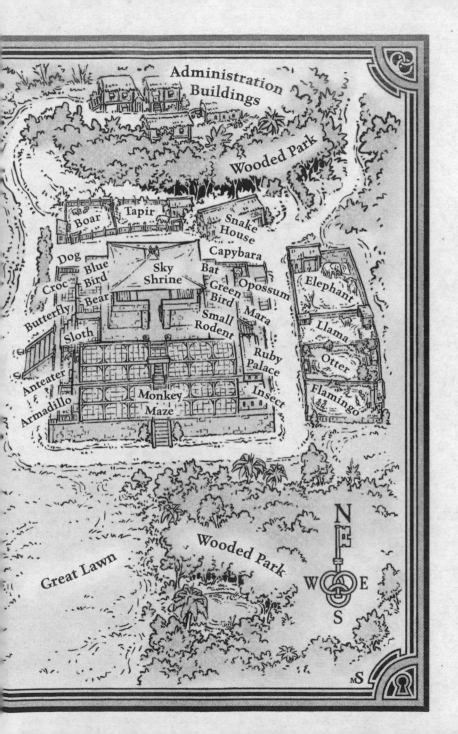

FIRST DAY

Happiest greetings and most vigorous welcomes to the Zoo at the Edge of the World. The most deliciously exotic, delightfully luxurious, and ravishingly beautiful resort on earth.

Your five-day, five-night, all-inclusive excursion starts this morning, the minute you step off the riverboat *Saint of the Animals*. We hope you're well rested.

You will be met at the dock by the resort's proprietor, Ronan Rackham. You will recognize him as the famous adventurer known the world over for his thrilling exploits in South America, but here the Conqueror of the Jungle is only your humble host.

Our courteous and experienced staff will spirit away your luggage, and all the stresses and strains of your travel will melt away. Take in a leisurely lunch or freshen up in your luxury accommodations. A Grand Tour of the grounds, gardens, and of course the zoo itself will take guests to the dining hour.

After dinner, the real fun begins. Don your finest dress and join your fellow guests at the Welcoming Gala.

As the happy natives say here in British Guiana: Join friends, and be honored!

I.

I woke up with a knot in my stomach that I couldn't pin on anything I'd eaten. For starters, no trumpet had sounded announcing Father's return from his hunt. And today was Greeting Day.

He'd never missed a Greeting Day before. I decided what I was feeling might be dread.

Father had warned us days ago that if he wasn't back in time, Tim and I were to run the festivities without him, but he assured us it wouldn't come to that. I wondered what was keeping him and whether he was safe.

I was useless on Greeting Day for reasons I'll soon get to, and with Tim as the older brother and all, that placed him in charge of my life.

Yes, it was definitely dread.

"Monkey Talker, you awake in there?" Tim shouted through the door, rattling the knob. Thank God for bedroom-door locks, or else big brothers might take over the world.

"You better not be sleeping, you little peeve!"

I wiped the night gunk from my eyes and tried to tell him to go away. My lips puckered together in spasm, and the air thickened up in my throat.

I winced, and "Guh—guh—ggg—gh!" is all that came out.

In the mornings, it sometimes takes a moment to remember I can't speak. I can always do it so easily in my dreams.

I gave up and instead rapped my knuckles against my bed frame to let him know I was awake.

"I expect you downstairs in five minutes. If you're late, I'll have you scooping up guano from the Bat House with a teaspoon."

Unmistakably dread.

Fortunately for me (though not for anyone within smelling distance), I'd slept in my work clothes. Yesterday's chores were written on my pants legs in dirt and dung, though I found a Brazil nut in my pant cuff and saved it for Kenji.

Tim was disappointed when I was down in under five minutes, and he told me I'd haul guano anyway.

"Demerits for dirty clothes. What kind of place do you think this is?"

"Ah zuh—zz-zuh . . ."

A zoo, I tried to say, but got stuck on the *z*.

I'm not a mute, and I'm not stupid like most people think.

What I am is a stutterer, and a bad one. I trip on the starts of words, my vowels get stuck, and *ums* wedge into everything. The only sound I can reliably get out is a sneeze.

I can manage a few words, sometimes, if the person I'm talking to is patient. Feeling rushed makes the stutter worse. I don't think Tim has ever stood still long enough for me to say hello, unless Father forced him.

"Sorry, no time for sound-it-out." He sneered. "We're needed at the boat. You'd be kept out of sight of the guests if it were up to me, but Father pities you. Come on."

As we marched down the hill from our house to the Golden Path, Tim kept stepping on the back of my shoe. If I tried to get away, he'd push me over and say it was an accident. So I let him have his fun.

The workers were out early today, sweeping the Golden Path and cleaning out cages. Everyone's up before dawn on Greeting Day, because everything has to be shined and lined up just right.

Tim, my father, and I spend so much time in the sun that you can barely tell the difference between us and the dark-skinned Arawaks and Caribs who are natives of this land and who we employ in the zoo. Guess the only thing is that my family all has wavy brown hair, while the natives' is thick, straight, and black. Or if you see us with our shirts off. We have monstrous tan lines.

Father puts the workers through their paces on Greeting Day, forbidding even a drop of dung in the animal cages. As though pooping isn't the main thing these creatures do.

"Spiff up that brick!" Tim shouted at a group of workers sweeping between the cages. "You're leaving it all spotty."

As much as Tim wanted to get to the boat quickly, he never passed up an opportunity to bark orders at someone. He jogged ahead a few yards and made the group double back up the path to sweep and mop as he supervised.

There was a tug at my pants leg, and I looked down to see a little mustachioed monkey scaling my thigh. She chirped and thrust her hand into my pocket.

"Kenji!" I knocked my knees together and grabbed her. "You sneaky thief! I saved this nut to give to you, not to have it swiped!"

Maybe I ought to explain. Up until now, I've cast myself as unable to speak. Well, I'll just say again, I am not a mute nor am I stupid. What I am is a stutterer. When I was small it was really bad. Tutors rejected me, saying I was hopeless. Father thought so too, and Tim still seems to think that way. But something changed when I turned five. Father heard of a Portuguese doctor passing through Georgetown, the capital city downriver from our zoo, who'd done studies on speech disorders. He arranged for an examination.

When you're a little kid and everyone's telling you you're dumb, it's hard not to believe them. And so that's what I thought, until I spoke to Dr. Vincente.

First, he said there was nothing wrong with my mind. I wasn't stupid. It was the way my mind worked with my lips, tongue, and lungs that caused the problem.

Second, he told me I was a stutterer and I'd always be a stutterer. But he taught me tricks I could use to improve my speech, how to improve my airflow and force my mouth into specific shapes.

As he was leaving, he told me one final thing. He said sometimes, a stutterer finds he may not stutter when he is alone and speaking to animals.

It sounds odd, I know, but it's true. The doctor suggested to my father that I be given a pet.

My father's name is Ronan Rackham, and he is an adventurer. He came to Guiana from England when he was just fourteen years old and never went back. He was the first Englishman to map the inland jungle, and he became famous for discovering new species of animals.

Heeding the doctor's advice, Father went into the jungle to fetch me a gift. He captured a white-and-gray tamarin monkey. She was the size of a small cat and had a red tail, beady eyes, and an enormous white mustache that grew wider than her face. She was a cute little girl, and while the zoo where I lived was filled with monkeys, I'd never had one as a pet before.

Remembering what Dr. Vincente said, I took her to my room and closed the door. There was a tiny corner I liked to hide in, between the wall and the bed, and we sat there together. I held the monkey under her arms. She blinked at me, curiously.

"I think I'll call you Kenji," I said.

My mouth snapped shut. I was five years old and I'd never said three words together before.

"Am I talking to you?" I asked. "I am!"

I hugged the little creature to my chest. She looked up at me pleasantly.

"I am talking to you," I said. "I can speak."

When the doctor told me I'd be able to speak, I'd allowed myself only a tiny bit of hope that it would be true. I told her the story of my entire life. Everything I thought of my brother and father, and everyone I'd ever met. I told her the plots of books Father read to me, and when I couldn't think of anything more to say, I told her my life story all over again.

At some point, Kenji and I fell asleep. The next day, Father found us in the corner behind the bed and woke me up.

I wanted to tell him the doctor was right. I could speak!

"Huh-hh-h—hhhh," is all that came out.

I was a stutterer and would always be a stutterer. The doctor never promised I could talk with another person.

But I could speak when I was alone with animals. And I've done so with the animals at the zoo for the last seven years.

The dawn sun was creeping over the treetops, giving everything a golden glow. I placed Kenji on my shoulder and gave her the Brazil nut.

"More where that came from," I said. "Greeting Day's today—we'll have a lot of new guests in. Show them your tricks and maybe you'll get an honest treat, instead of having to steal one."

But Kenji already had her hand in my shirt pocket, tickling me and fishing around for more.

2.

There was a metallic clatter in the pen to my left, and then a powerful snort.

Leedo Flute flipped himself over the railing of the Boar Den and rolled onto the Golden Path. He looked at me, spit, and then walked away.

Leedo is one of our native workers, and he must have had a tangle with Tuskus, our male forest boar. Tuskus had never liked Leedo, who held his dung shovel in the air like a meat cleaver, scaring the boars. Leedo wouldn't pay attention when I tried to show him the proper way.

Father might be back that afternoon, and if the Boar Den wasn't clean, there'd be a price to pay. So I unlocked the door to the den and found the shovel lying in the muddy pit. When I picked it up, I was sure to hold the blade downward like I was stirring a kettle of awful-smelling soup.

Tuskus lifted his head and snorted at me. He quickly

trotted between me and the two female boars, Gray Beard and Belly Wart. Tuskus is very protective of those two.

"It's your poop I'm after," I said. "Not your girlfriends."

I went about my business clearing his business, and Tuskus began circling me. I let him sniff at my pants legs and shirt while Kenji hung tight to my neck, keeping a cautious eye on the boar. Finally, Tuskus whined and pressed his cheek against my thigh. I scratched his forehead and he grunted happily.

He's a piglet at heart. It's just that most people can't see past the eight-inch tusks we've named him for. I can't say I blame them for that.

"You stinky thing!" I said, as a great bubble of spit slimed its way onto my pants leg. "I come in here to get you cleaned up, and look what you duh-dd-d—"

The words caught in my throat. I saw Leedo leaning over the fence, leering at me.

"Make friends with a pig, smell like a pig." He laughed.

I kept shoveling.

"How come you talk to animals but you won't talk to me, little Marlin?"

I didn't look up.

"Why's your brother making us clean everything when the boss isn't even back yet?" Leedo leaned over the fence and picked up a clump of wet dirt. He crumpled it between his reedy fingers. "Maybe the boss isn't coming back."

I stuck the shovel in the ground and faced him. Leedo

was, without question, my least favorite employee. He was rude to the guests and always late with his duties. But no matter how often Tim complained, Father would never fire him. Father would say that everyone was good at something.

"He's c-cc-cuh-cuh—" *He's coming back,* I tried to say, but immediately regretted it.

"What's that, little Marlin?" Leedo laughed. "I don't speak your language."

I felt blood rush to my face. I wanted to take the shovel out of the ground and slap him on the side of the head with it.

"Hunting jaguar is not like hunting a little boar," Leedo continued, throwing a clump of dirt at Tuskus's head. It spooked him and he jumped up snorting. "When you hunt a jaguar, he hunts you right back."

I thought about opening the gate and letting Tuskus have his way with Leedo. But that wouldn't be the right thing to do. Father was counting on Tim and me to act responsibly in his stead.

So I picked up the shovel and got back to work. Behind me Leedo cursed and walked off. *My father is Ronan Rackham,* I thought; *he is smarter and stronger than anything on earth. No one can kill him.*

Or so I hoped.

It was our employees' fault that Father had to risk his life in the first place. Our zoo is built on an ancient pyramid, and we'd turned every part of it into an attraction except for one: the Sky Shrine. The biggest and highest point on the pyramid is set up like a stadium, with a large pit surrounded by stone benches. Father thought it would be an excellent place to make a circus ring and put on animal shows.

Construction was going fine until one of our cage keepers, Nathtam Leent, told everyone a seer from the Tribes had claimed the Sky Shrine was holy and it was sacrilege to make a circus there. "The Tribes" is what we call the various communities of Arawaks and Caribs that still live in their villages and do things the old way. Most of our employees are former Tribesmen as well, so Father gives the native communities respect. He even bought the fabric for the circus tent from the Tribes. That's how they learned what he was up to.

We raised the tent last week, and Nathtam led a third of our employees on strike and into the jungle. They planned to rejoin the Tribesmen there.

Father was as angry about this as I had ever seen him. He was missing all through dinner and then appeared at my bedroom door at midnight, his eyes like stone.

The circus was going to be the most impressive part of the resort, Father told me, the centerpiece of the new zoo experience. It was the reason he would be able to raise the fees he was charging the guests for the coming season. He said he'd made some very expensive land deals recently, and if we had to close the resort for even one week, it could be disastrous.

I didn't sleep well that night, fearing our zoo would close. All the animals would be released into the jungle, and I would have to return to Georgetown. I'd lose my friends and have only Kenji to talk to.

But the next morning our striking workers were waiting at the gate. They were all there, except for one.

They had made camp in the jungle that first night, but after sunset Nathtam had gone missing. It was a moonless night, and they couldn't search for him until morning.

The found him just after sunrise. He was hanging from a tree. Or part of him was.

A jaguar had got to him.

When a jaguar turns man-eater, he learns a bad lesson: people taste good and are easy to catch. Whole tribal villages had been terrorized when a jaguar learned to hunt humans. That's why the workers came back. They needed the protection of our walls—the protection only my father could provide.

Father opened our gates to the men, and let them have their jobs and quarters back with no punishments. When they feared for the safety of their families still living in the villages, Father told them he'd go out and kill the man-eater himself.

"We are Rackham men," he told Tim and me. "And Rackhams always do what's right."

3.

Tim and I were at the boat only to greet the guests, but the employees did all the work, carrying luggage and directing everyone to their carriages. Father would usually make a big show of taking one guest's luggage personally, often that of the most important visitor. Some of the richest and most powerful people in the world come to our resort. I've seen Father's account books, and what these guests pay for a week's vacation could get you a modest house in Georgetown.

As the guests came off the boat, Tim leaped right into Father's shoes, complimenting the sweating ladies on their beauty and slapping the overstuffed gentlemen on their backs. A wet sound, that slap. These rich ladies and gentlemen have no sense of proper jungle wear.

A lady in a drooping red hat tapped her husband on the shoulder and whispered, "That's them, right behind us!"

The couple stepped to the side of the gangplank and made a deep bow, and the other guests around them followed suit. I looked for the people they were talking about, but before I could see, Tim nearly pushed me over, pressing down my head.

When I looked back up, a family of three was slowly making their way toward the dock. The first was a giant white-haired man whose beard radiated from his cheeks into two perfect corners below his ears. He wore a dazzling vest with what looked like actual silver thread woven into the fabric. A gold watch peeked up from his pocket. His manner was stately and regal and was betrayed only by the fact that his linen pants were so soaked with sweat, it looked like he'd just sat in a bathtub.

Next to him strode a tall, elegant woman who I assumed was his wife. Her beauty was so striking, I hardly noticed the rouge and mascara melting down her face in the heat.

And in front of them was a girl. At first glance I took her for a servant, because she was so out of line with the other two in both pace and demeanor. She walked with a broad step and had hitched up her dress and rolled up her sleeves to keep cool. I'd never seen a guest do that right off the boat before when they were still trying to impress the other guests.

She also didn't have the melting makeup problem, because she wore none.

"Duke, Duchess." Tim stepped between the family and me, and bowed. Then he turned to the girl, who looked about my age, twelve or thirteen. "Lady Bradshire. I am Timothy Rackham, and I bid all of you welcome to the Zoo at the Edge of the World. Allow me to take your bags."

Tim reached out his hand and grabbed an ornate bag from the porter.

"What a gentleman!" the duchess cooed.

"You, my boy," said the duke as he shook Tim's unencumbered hand, "are the very image of your father."

I'd heard we had some noble family coming this week. Father said he knew the Duke of Bradshire from his brief time in the navy and that he'd be bringing his wife. He didn't say anything to me about the daughter.

"And you're a Rackham, too?" The girl pushed past Tim and curtsied for me. "You're all famous back in England, you know."

"Yes, that's my younger brother, Marlin," Tim said, smiling through his teeth.

"Oh!" she said, tittering. "You have no idea how boring life is back there. What's it like to be an adventurer?"

She was speaking directly to me. None of the guests ever spoke directly to me. Her eyes were green and so innocent in their inquiring that I could tell she actually expected an answer. The last thing I wanted to do was stutter in her pretty face.

"That's the dullard son," the Duchess of Bradshire whispered behind her hand loudly enough for everyone to hear. She gave me a squinting smile through her melted makeup.

The girl looked embarrassed and dropped her eyes.

A weight smacked my chest and I reflexively grabbed it. Tim had shoved the duke's bag at me and was fighting with the devil to contain his laughter. He just managed to choke out, "Show them to their carriage," before bolting off in a hysterical fit behind a donkey.

I slowly lifted my chin from the bag but made no eye contact with the duke and his family. I nodded in the direction of their carriage and led the way forward.

The length of boardwalk from the gangplank to the duke's carriage was short, but the bag was large; even with my arms wrapped around it, my hands barely touched. It was a struggle to open the door without losing my grip on the bag. Once the bag was safely inside, I stepped back, bowed, and gestured for the duke's family to enter. One by one I watched their feet walk by, until their daughter's knobby knees stopped in front of my view.

I kept my head bowed until she tapped my shoulder.

"Would you like to ride with us?" she asked.

Tim reappeared from behind the donkey. "That's not customary," he said. "We walk up."

The girl smiled at Tim. "He brought our bag to the carriage; why not see it the rest of the way?"

The dumfounded look on my brother's face was delicious, and I wish I'd had more time to enjoy it, but as soon as she'd dismissed him, the girl took my arm and pulled me into the carriage with her parents. The door swung shut behind me, and then I was there with the Bradshire family, nobility of a country I'd never seen.

"Let the boy go about his business," said the duke.

"What better business does he have than getting acquainted with us?" his daughter replied. "We are his guests, after all."

With that she knocked twice on the wall of the carriage, and the driver set off.

We hit a bump, and the duchess nearly fell out of her seat. "You behave yourself on this trip, young lady," she tried to scold the girl, but between the streaks of red and black makeup on her face and the way she clung to the walls of the carriage, she was hard to take seriously.

"Don't be so stiff, Mummy," her daughter chided. "We're here to have an adventure!"

The duchess considered her grimly. Adventuring, I wagered, was not her cup of tea.

The girl looked at me happily from the opposite bench and squinted as though she were puzzling me out.

"My name is Olivia," she said.

"Lady Olivia," corrected the duke.

"Oh, you don't need to say that part among friends. What's your name? I don't think I got it."

"Livia! Stop torturing that boy," said the duke as he tried to steady himself in the bouncing carriage. "He's a mute."

My face heated up. Olivia looked away to hide her disappointment.

I closed my eyes and remembered the techniques the speech doctor had taught me in Georgetown. *Lips, tongue, teeth, air. I am not a mute.*

"Mmm-mm—muh, ma ma," I stuttered, and stopped.

The duke huffed, and the duchess shot a knowing look toward her husband. But Olivia sat still and considered me calmly. I started again, deliberately working the mechanics of my mouth.

"MM-mm—MUH—MUH—Marlin," I managed.

Olivia smiled. "Marlin! Good to meet you." She took my hand in hers and very enthusiastically shook it. Her hands were much softer than mine, and way more clean.

"I can't believe I'm actually meeting the world-famous Rackhams! This is my very first time in South America," she said. "Daddy's here to buy land for a sugar forest. He says we might move here!"

The duchess kicked Olivia in the shin from across the carriage.

"Ow!" she cried.

The duke stiffened up. "I'm not sure where my daughter comes up with these stories."

Olivia opened her mouth to say something but seemed to think better of it, and sighed.

My father was born to a wealthy family like the Bradshires back in England, but he hated the stodgy life he led there. He longed for adventure in the colonies. So first chance he got, he hopped a ship for Guiana, Britain's colony on the South American mainland. But in the port city of Georgetown he found men not too different from the ones he was fleeing in England: merchants and landowners obsessed with reaping riches from the mines and sugarcane plantations around the coast. He spent the next thirty years traveling the jungles of the Amazon and writing dispatches for British newspapers.

On a rare visit to Georgetown, he met Marion Coates, the daughter of a ship's captain. They fell in love and she convinced him to give up his adventuring and settle in the city. They lived there together for three years, very happily. But Marion, my mother, died of illness soon after I was born. Neither Tim nor I have any memory of her.

Father wrote to his brother back in England with instructions to sell his estate there, and he used the money to move us upriver and into the jungle. That's where he built this resort, the Zoo at the Edge of the World.

The idea was to make a destination for the rich merchants in Georgetown, demonstrating the beauty of the natural world. But I suppose it caught the attention of the wealthy back in England as well, because soon loads of them were boarding steamships bound for South America just to visit us.

I can't tell you if we're famous or not, but the resort is always booked.

"Daddy, look!" Olivia squealed as the carriage pulled onto the Golden Path. "The Grand Gate! It's even better than in the books!"

4.

Sometimes I wonder why people who speak the most always seem to have the least to say.

The guests had had their tea and changed into more reasonable clothes, and were now being led around the grounds of the resort by Tim. He was pretty much bungling the whole thing.

"Our zoo is built on the ruins of a stone pyramid that is over one hundred years old," Tim prattled to the assembled guests.

Over one hundred years old is technically correct, but the pyramid is actually over *seven* hundred years old.

"There are more than thirty different species of animals in our zoo," he went on, leading the group down the Golden Path.

We have exactly eighty-seven species in our collection.

The great stone pyramid on which our zoo rests was a

temple complex built by the native people in ancient times. There was once a great city here, and they built this pyramid as a tribute to their gods. Steps run up the pyramid on all four sides, and along those steps are dozens of shrines and chambers stacked all the way to the pinnacle.

The city must have been abandoned some time ago, because the jungle swallowed it up, leaving only the pyramid. Some of the structures along the temple shelf remained intact, while some were just pillars and fallen stone.

My father discovered the site on one of his first expeditions. It's about fifty miles inland from Georgetown, but there is no road through this dense jungle, so the only way to get here is by our riverboat, *Saint of the Animals*.

Old shrines and chambers along the pyramid were fitted with bars to make them suitable as animal enclosures. My father captured most of the animals himself in the surrounding forest; the rest were shipped in from Africa and the Caribbean. The pyramid is nearly a half mile square, but not very steep, so it's easy to walk the steps between the different animal attractions. We call the steps and the paths around the zoo the Golden Path, because the bricks are made from a kind of mud that hardens with a yellow hue.

Tim led the snaking group of guests up and down the Golden Path, all the time providing them with more misinformation.

"And on your left you'll see Crocodile Corner," Tim called out, "a stone enclosure where we keep three

23

full-grown crocs"—*two adults and a baby, in truth*—"one of which I caught myself."

Not a chance.

"Caught a crocodile!" The duchess tittered to Olivia. "That's a boy you want to get acquainted with."

Olivia blushed and smiled. She looked over at me, and I couldn't help shaking my head, as if to say, *It's not true.*

I suppose I was jealous.

"Why are you shaking your head?" she whispered.

"Huh—hh-hh—h," I stammered. *He didn't catch a crocodile!* I wanted to say.

But I couldn't. I never could. And so I stepped off the Golden Path and, with a quick flick of my hand, bade Olivia to follow me.

I took her on my own tour of the zoo and showed off my favorite animals. I showed her Longsnout and Bottlebee at the Tapir Pond, Minxy in the Sloth Cage, and Mala, the spectacled bear. All without words, of course; when she asked questions, I kept it to a shake or a nod. I wanted to tell her all the things I knew about the animals. I had funny stories about each creature, but I was afraid if I stuttered I'd look a fool.

We ended up at the Elephant Stomping Grounds to visit Dreyfus, our big gray. He was shipped over from Africa when he was just a youngling, and he'd had a major growth spurt recently.

I wanted to tell Olivia he'd nearly doubled his body

weight in three months. But I wouldn't risk bungling the words.

"My God!" Olivia exclaimed as we came within sight. "It's an elephant!" She grabbed my collar in shock. "An elephant!" she said again.

I laughed. Most English hadn't seen half the animals we've got in their shoddy zoos. It's always fun to watch a guest's first encounter with a creature.

"He's marvelous!" Olivia moved toward the gate. "His trunk can move just like an arm! In all the books it's a dragging, hanging thing."

Dreyfus was picking some greens out of a trough with his trunk and shoving them into his mouth. A two-ton beast that uses his nose like a hand was so commonplace to me that it took a moment to see what was so fascinating about it.

"How much does he weigh?" she inquired of me. Her face was alight with joy.

I opened my mouth without thinking and stammered. "Whoo—whoo—whaaaaa-"

My hand covered my mouth and stopped the noise. Olivia's smile wavered for a moment.

"He must weigh quite a lot," she said.

All my stories were stopped up inside. Tim would have been a better guide: even with all his rubbish, he always had something to say.

Olivia leaned against the gate, pressing her face between the bars.

"Mr. Elephant . . . ," she cooed. "Mr. Funny Elephant, what are you munching on?"

Dreyfus looked up from his feed trough and trumpeted.

"Nothing for me, I guess!" Olivia laughed uproariously.

At that moment, I realized there was something I could do. I gestured for her to step away from the gate, and I pulled the brass key ring off my belt.

"Marlin, what are you doing?"

I smiled and found the key I needed. I opened the big creaky gate just enough to squeeze through. Dreyfus was easy to spook, so I closed the gate behind me and crept toward him to check his mood.

The big elephant was back at his trough in the center of the stomping grounds. He eyed me cautiously but kept on chewing. We were out of earshot of Olivia and I felt my tongue relax, my breath returning to my throat.

"Hello, pal." I stroked his trunk. "I've got a visitor for you, if that's all right. She's a girl." I dropped down to a whisper. "And she's pretty nice. I think she'd like it very much if she could give you a pat. What do you say?"

Dreyfus considered me from above, then went back to munching. I took that as a *yes.*

Olivia called to me, "Everything all right there, Marlin?"

I smiled broadly and waved her in. She pushed the gate slightly open and squeezed through. Perhaps too optimistically, she skipped toward Dreyfus, and I felt him shift his weight. Before I could tell her to slow down, she came right up to him and hugged his trunk like a pet.

I winced and braced myself for the worst, but the elephant just snorted and went on eating. "He's a gentle giant!" Olivia laughed, and I couldn't help joining her. "This is wonderful, Marlin. Thank you so much—"

A bugling sound blasted through the air. Dreyfus reared up his head, and Olivia, still embracing his trunk, went up with it. She screamed and tumbled into the mud.

I ran to help her up and another bugle blast sounded.

"I'm all right," she said, standing up from the mud. "What were those trumpets?"

I pulled her toward the elephant gate. I'd get in trouble if someone found us here. We weren't supposed to bring guests into the enclosures. It was Father's number one rule.

"Marlin, what is it?" she asked again as I locked the gate and dragged her toward the Golden Path.

"MM—mm—MU-muh—MMMM—" My tongue thickened up.

I pointed my index finger horizontal and set it beneath my nose.

"A mustache?" Olivia looked puzzled.

I straightened up and puffed my chest.

"Your father!" she guessed. She must have seen an engraving of him somewhere.

I nodded and pulled her desperately back toward the group, praying he wouldn't find out I'd left.

5.

We spotted the rest of the guests heading down the bottom of the Golden Path on their way to the gatehouse. Some of them had already gathered outside the door.

"What are they all doing?" Olivia asked me.

I had no idea. The gatehouse was a small building attached to a stable where we housed donkeys. There was no reason for guests to be there.

"Livia!" the duchess shrieked when she saw us. "What happened to you?"

"What's going on?" Olivia asked.

"You tell me, young lady. You're covered in mud!"

"Oh my goodness, you're right." Olivia feigned surprise.

"You were with *him*." The duchess snapped her fingers in my face. "Boy! Boy!"

"He's not deaf, Mother," Olivia said.

"Well, then he should be able to hear this clearly," the duchess pronounced. Her face was sharp and beautiful, and very frightening when she was angry. "Stay away from my daughter."

"Daddy!" Olivia turned to her father, who had been standing by ineffectually. For such a large and powerful man, he didn't seem quite equipped to deal with an argument between the duchess and Olivia.

"Oh, Everly, there's no need to be harsh," the duke offered. "This boy doesn't know what you're saying."

"Yes, he does!" Olivia said, now angry at both her parents.

I'd just been screamed at, insulted, and argued over in the space of about a minute, and I still had my own family to worry about. I decided it'd be best to bid the Bradshires farewell.

"Buh—bb-buh-buh—" I stammered as a means of excusing myself, and made all the necessary bows as quickly as I could.

"I'm sorry, Marlin," Olivia mouthed as I waved and backed away. I nodded to show everything was fine but decided I wouldn't be talking to her anytime soon. It was always best to leave the guests alone. Though I did need to push through a horde of them to get to the gatehouse.

"Little Marlin," said Leedo Flute, who was guarding the door, "they just dragged your father back here on a gurney. Guess the jaguar got him after all."

A hollow pain opened in my chest. "Wh-wh-WH-what?" I gasped.

Leedo's grim face was beset by twitching. His right eye wrinkled involuntarily and his lip jerked up.

"Bah-ha-ha-ha!" he laughed uproariously. My face soured and I pushed him hard in the gut. He grabbed my arm with his strong, thin hands and easily tossed me to the side.

"I'm only joking, little Marlin. He's right inside there and has been asking for you about a quarter of an hour. Where have you been?"

I pushed by him and through the wide wooden door. Leedo slammed it shut behind me.

Ronan Rackham turned around, his face tensed and eyes wide. All the nights in the bush had ravaged his nerves, and loud noises tended to startle him. I always thought of it as his Jungle Look.

Several days of stubble was shading his chin, and sweat from his forehead streamed into a bushy mustache. The khaki sleeves on his shirt were rolled up, and I could see the thick forearm veins that popped out even when he held a teacup.

My father was an old man. He had turned sixty just last winter, but he looked like men half his age. The only place his years showed was in the wrinkles near his eyes when he smiled. He liked to say that he'd lived an entire life before having children, and Tim and I were his second life.

The Jungle Look melted into a smile.

"Marlin!" he bellowed. "Where have you been?"

"Ay-ay-uh-uh-uh," I stuttered.

"Yes, where were you?" repeated Tim with a smirk, trying to start trouble. "Tell us."

Father ignored him. He pulled me close and mussed my hair with a dirty hand. Then he hooked both our heads into his elbows and drew us into his chest. "Boys, boys, boys!" he chanted as he smothered us in his shirt. We gasped for breath and giggled, relieved at his good mood. "You would have been eaten alive out there!"

Tim and I broke free and we mock battled him, punching his arms and shoulders as he pressed us backward by our necks.

"I wish you two had been with me," he said. "You'd be dead, of course, but it would have been a nice way to die."

"So you killed the jaguar?" Tim said, grabbing hold of his arm. "Can I have its skull?"

"Well . . ." Father gave us a small smile and glanced at Manray Lightfoot, one of our newer employees, who was carrying a chain into the gatehouse stable. "First I want to see that Paw. Have it out!"

The Paw. He never told us where he got it, or what it was, but that never mattered. It was a dry and crusty thing that looked something like a lemur's hand. Its tiny knuckles were balled up in a fist. The thing was ghastly to look at, and it smelled awful. But I would do anything to have it.

31

"Right here," Tim said, and pulled it out of his breast pocket. Tim always kept it close when he had it, which was most of the time.

"Good," Father said. "We're about to have a game."

Sometimes Father challenged us to do something that required bravery or smarts. The winner got to hold the Paw until he did something especially bad or the other one did something especially good. Then it was transferred again.

I usually got it only when Tim did something bad, and then I'd quickly lose it; I never had it for more than a day, because Tim won most of the games. He was stronger, faster, and braver. Plus he could talk.

"What's the game?" Tim asked excitedly. He'd had the Paw for the last two weeks straight. I tried not to drive myself crazy by counting, but Tim kept a count, and made sure I was duly informed every evening at dinner.

"The game is afoot," Father said, snatching the Paw from Tim. "And closer than you think."

Just then the door banged open.

"Mr. Rackham," Leedo complained. "it's mad out here!"

"Captain Rackham!" the guests called out. "Captain Rackham!"

"What do you want me to do?" Leedo threw up his arms.

Father gave us a knowing look. "Slight pause for interference," he said. "We mustn't leave a bunch of sweaty snobs waiting."

"Yes, Father. You should go out there," Tim said, feigning

worry. "I tried to control the group as best I could, but Marlin abandoned us when we were on the tour, and it wasn't easy leading the whole thing by myself."

He threw me under the carriage, the tattler. I tried to put together a statement in my mind explaining my absence in the fewest words possible, leaving out the bit about letting a guest be mauled by an elephant, of course.

But Father casually patted Tim on the shoulder and said with exaggerated patience, "You get better with experience."

Then he winked at me and walked to the gatehouse door.

Tim's jaw dropped. I knew he'd make me pay for it later, but it was worth it.

The gatehouse door opened and the red setting sun blazed behind the crowd, casting everyone in silhouette. They waved and called out, "Captain Rackham! Captain Rackham!" pushing each other for a better look. This was always my favorite part of Greeting Day. A special pride welled up in me, hearing them cheer him. Tim and I stood to either side of our father, soaking up all the glory we could.

"Hello and welcome," Father said quietly. "Thank you all for journeying to our zoo." Immediately the chattering crowd went silent. I'd seen him use this trick before. Father never had to shout to get attention. "I'm so sorry that I wasn't able to greet you properly at the docks. But I trust that my sons Marlin and Timothy hosted you admirably."

Tim blinked hard and his mouth twitched. Father had said my name first.

"I would have joined you," he went on, "but my latest expedition went on longer than I hoped. I promise I'll make it up to you with the wonderful—"

"Another adventure, Captain?" a voice called from the crowd.

Father furrowed his brow and searched the silhouettes for the source of this interruption. A large, round, familiar shape separated itself from the others and approached us.

Slowly, Father unknitted his brow and curled his lips into what had all the features of a smile but was missing some vital ingredient.

"Your Grace," Father said through his teeth, and dipped into a deep bow. The guests near the gatehouse bowed and tipped their hats too. The duke's smile was genuine, and he laughed and waved at the guests.

"Good to see you, Admiral," Father said stiffly. "And Your Grace. So many titles now, hard to choose just one."

Guests in the crowd chuckled at this.

"I've brought my family with me!" the duke said loudly, as if he were onstage and performing a show for the other guests. He gestured to one short and one tall silhouette to my right. "Let me introduce my wife, Everly, the Duchess of Bradshire, and my daughter, Lady Olivia."

Olivia and her mother made their entrances like they were accustomed to this sort of thing. They came to the front of the gatehouse and curtsied first to the crowd and then to my father. The duchess refused to make eye contact with any of us, but Olivia shot me a smile. My plan to avoid Olivia and the Bradshires was not off to a good start. But I smiled to let her know I was enjoying her mother's discomfort as well.

"And these are my sons, once again, Timothy and Marlin," Father said flatly. We looked at each other, not knowing what to do, until Father pinched us. Then we bowed.

"Beauties and the Beasts!" a guest wearing a green driving jacket called out. The duke chuckled at this, and the rest of the group followed suit. I suppose our two families together did make quite a sight. One was the height of English society, and the other made a living running a zoo in the jungle. But Olivia, in her muddy dress, looked like she belonged more with our lot.

"We're delighted to be here," the duke said.

"And delighted you're still in business," added the duchess while looking over my father's shoulder.

"Why wouldn't we still be in business?" Father bristled.

"It's a lovely resort, Captain Rackham," interjected the duke. "Even more grand than in the pamphlets we've seen. We are just delighted to be here and—"

"You'll have to excuse us, Your Grace," Father said, much louder than necessary. "And to you all, I apologize as well, but I have urgent business to attend with my sons." He shot me a look. "I will properly greet you tonight at the Welcoming Gala. Leedo, please show the guests to their cabins."

Leedo sighed with exasperation, and Father gave him a quick kick in the shin.

"Captain—" the duke protested, but Father pretended he didn't hear and pushed Tim and me back into the gatehouse. Leedo was unenthusiastically addressing the crowd as the door closed.

"England not big enough for them?" Father said to himself. "Have to lord over my land as well?"

He spun violently and punched the wall, cracking it.

Tim and I jumped back and locked eyes. Father stayed facing the damaged wall. I watched his enormous shoulders rise and fall as he breathed. Never once had Father turned his strength on either of us, but I'd seen him crack enough walls to imagine what it'd feel like.

"Don't mind me, boys," Father said. "Just a bit of business between me and that one is all. Come on, now." Father slapped our backs. "Game's afoot, and it's a good one."

6.

Slivers of light leaked from the roof into the stable, and my eyes took their time adjusting. I saw only dim outlines in the room, sweat gleaming off the shoulder of a worker, maybe Manray, as he walked by.

He was dragging a heavy chain across the floor, and I could hear the sound of metal pieces coming unsettled and then clinking back together.

"Do you see him?" Father whispered.

"See what?" Tim asked.

"Over there." Father pointed. "The end of the stable."

Tim went absolutely frozen. He must have seen it before I did.

"Wuh—wuh-ww—" My eyes were just beginning to make out a shape.

"Holy . . ." Tim gasped. "You said you were going to kill it!"

Father laughed, loud and hard. It made me jump. When I opened my eyes again, it became clear to me.

"Our newest attraction!" Father said.

The shadows at the end of the stable coalesced, and I could see the black outline of bars on a mobile carrier. The wheeled cage was parked at the far wall of the room, and inside it was a smoothly flowing shadow.

I couldn't tell one end of the undulating mass from the other until it opened its eyes. Yellow orbs blinked at me.

"W—w—whu—why?" I managed to ask Father.

"Why bring it back alive?" Father said, and I nodded. "Why not, I ask you?"

"He's a man-eater," Tim blurted out.

Father tipped his head. "That's true," he said. "The beast did kill Nathtam. And with a taste for human flesh, it's not safe for him to be roaming around."

"But then why'd you bring him here?"

Father turned to me to gauge my reaction. I couldn't hide that I wondered it too. Across the room, the jaguar snarled.

"The beast doesn't abide by our rules, only the rules of the jungle. He ate a man because a man put himself in his way," Father said. "I'm not happy about what happened, but I won't punish an animal for being an animal. Would you?"

Tim mumbled a nothing, and I shrugged.

"That's not why we're here, my boys. This zoo isn't just entertainment for the rich. We are showing that the wilds of the jungle can be conquered. That there is nothing to fear. Anyone can come here and enjoy these lands."

"Yes, Father," Tim said dutifully.

"Yeh-ye—yes," I said. I couldn't argue with what Father had said. The jaguar was just an animal, doing what animals do. Even if it scared me.

"But if we want to show the world there's nothing to fear," Father said, motioning Manray over, "we must be fearless ourselves."

Manray handed him two collar sticks, long metal rods, each with an adjustable noose at the end. "First one to collar him gets the Paw," Father said, urging us forward.

"Are you serious?" Tim gasped, pushing back toward Father.

"Are you chicken?" Father laughed. "What about you, Marlin?"

Tim shot me an uncertain look. If we both refused the challenge, the game would be canceled and he could keep the Paw. I could avoid the shame of losing and stay far from the jaguar. But I didn't know when I'd have another chance to win it.

I took the collar stick and started creeping toward the cage.

"Oh, curse it!" Tim griped, grabbing the other collar stick and coming up behind me. "You said you'd kill this bloody thing!"

"And miss this entertainment?" Father bellowed. "I've never made a better decision in my life."

Tim came up beside me, and we advanced toward the cage with our shoulders touching. If he'd wanted to be first, he could have easily sped ahead of me, but we were both near petrified. If Father hadn't been watching, I think we might have crawled. Or run away entirely.

The outline of the creature's form filled in, and his terrible proportions became clear. The chest was narrow, and his limbs were lithe and thin. Enormous pads with two-inch claws capped each foot, and his mouth was wide with teeth.

The jaguar sat up straight and towered over Tim and me. We both sweatily gripped our collar sticks. I looked to Tim, but he pretended not to notice, focusing only on the jaguar.

Its yellow eyes rolled from him to me, like moons migrating across the sky.

"Give it a try, Marlin," Father called. "Tim's froze up."

That did it. With a thrust, Tim shot his collar stick between the iron bars of the cage. The jaguar leaped back and the carrier shifted, causing the bars to tilt with the swaying ceiling.

Tim swiped the noose and missed. The jaguar pressed the rod against the bottom of the cage with his paw, bit down on it, and with one powerful flick of his neck pulled it all the way into the cage, then out between the bars on the other side.

Tim's collar stick landed in a pile of donkey droppings. His hands were red from where the slipping of the rod had burned him.

"Going to try it again?" Father laughed.

Tim tensed his lips and looked back at him. "Marlin should have to try first."

I adjusted the rod in my hand and glanced at Tim, who was backing away from the cage toward the safety of the wall.

The jaguar and I locked eyes, and a low grumble emitted from his throat. I couldn't tell if it was a growl or a purr.

I gingerly slid the noose end of the rod between the bars of the carrier, keeping it low and nonthreatening.

"That's it, Marlin," Father mumbled from behind. "Easy does it."

Gradually, I lifted the collar end of the stick off the cage floor and pressed it gently against the side of the jaguar's foreleg. I left it there for a moment, applying slight pressure, to let the jaguar become acquainted with the collar and show him there was nothing to fear.

The jaguar kept his head high, glancing down at me. I would have said he had a bemused expression on his face, if an animal could be bemused.

I lifted the noose end of the rod higher, tracing the outline of the jaguar's form upward. Through the pressure I put on the rod, it was almost like I was petting him, and I could feel the remarkable firmness of the creature's muscles. Though slim, he was strong.

The noose went over his head like a collar over a dog's. I turned the knob that tightened the cord, and the job was done.

"Yes!" Father said from the end of the stable. "Well done, Marlin!"

"It wasn't that still for me," Tim griped. "That's not fair."

"Just make sure it's tight," Father said, ignoring Tim.

I put my hand on the knob, having intentionally left some slack. But I turned it tighter, and the jaguar gurgled in his throat.

"Sorry," I whispered to the jaguar, Father still out of earshot. "Does that hurt?"

The jaguar's eyes flashed and the beast yanked back his head with enough force that the rod, and my arms trailing with it, rammed between two bars of the cage.

I let go of the stick, but my arms were stuck in the bars, exposed to his claws and his teeth. Once jaguars bite, they don't let go. His cold nose sniffed up my forearms until the bars separated our faces by mere inches.

Then he roared.

Father caught me at the chest, and my arms wrenched out of the cage as I tumbled to the floor. There were shouts and growls, and my feet went *tut-tut-tut* against the stones as Father dragged me away. I couldn't do anything but smell the stench of his armpit and feel the throbbing in my head.

The world around me went cloudy and muffled and dark. But I paid no attention. There was only one thought in my mind.

The jaguar had told me, "Yes."

FIRST NIGHT

The Zoo at the Edge of the World is famous for attracting high-class clientele, and nowhere is the exquisite breeding of our guests on finer display than at the Welcoming Gala.

Lords and ladies from every corner of the Commonwealth and Europe have graced the dance floor of our Great Hall. Once an Italian prince bought up all of one week's tickets and brought his entire court along for the fun.

We are surrounded by savage jungle, but our Great Hall is pure high-society. Make sure you take time to admire the Chinese dinnerware and French stained-glass windows.

Your master of ceremonies, Captain Ronan Rackham, has a soft spot for the sweet sounds of England, and they are played magnificently by our house band.

After you've glided across our white-tile dance floor in the arms of your beloved, swaying to the nostalgic strains of a heavenly tune, you'll swear you're not in the Americas at all, but instead dancing the night away at the royal palace.

7

I could hear someone talking through the walls.

"The big man's back."

I'd been lying awake for hours, running the events of the day through my head. Father took me out the back door of the gatehouse with Manray. When we got back to our house, I told him I was fine. That's when he gave me the Paw. Tim was furious and said I screwed up and almost got myself killed so I shouldn't have it. But Father said he was proud of me.

We ate and washed and prepared for the Welcoming Gala, which I usually loved. But that night, the music seemed muted, the food tasted bland, and I couldn't focus on a single thing anybody said or did all night.

Because the jaguar told me, "Yes."

But now there was someone in our house, and I was scared.

"Just be quick about it."

"You think they're asleep?"

Robbers are dangerous out here. No policemen, no protection. We post guards around the walls of the resort at night, but there's no one at our home; Father prefers privacy. The men are always saying he should post a guard at the door. Lots of criminals from Georgetown hide out in the jungle, and this is a good place to sack, filled with rich guests.

"It's getting late. We should make a move."

I flung off the sheets. The night air was cool and it raised bumps on my skin. If they were in the house already, it might be too late.

"Go and tell us if it's clear."

I put my hand to the Paw in my front pajama pocket, and it gave me courage. I leaped out of bed, ran to the big door at the end of the hall, and frantically knocked.

On the other side, I heard a curse and the sound of a turning lock. Father opened the door in sleeping clothes. His hairy legs were bare beneath white shorts, his eyes squinty, and his mustache flattened on the side he'd been sleeping on.

He collared me and closed the door behind us, opening the oil lamp he kept hanging from the bedpost and turning the spark stone. A golden light leaped across the room.

46

A big bronze ring that hung on an iron hook glowed brightly. They were Father's keys to the zoo. He ran his fingers over them and sat across from me.

"Sound it out slow," he said.

"RR—rh—rh-rh—" I stuttered, and stopped. Father seemed patient tonight, or maybe he was still just half asleep. I minded my mouth contacts. *Lips, tongue, teeth, air.* "RR—ro—oo—"

It hurt. My lips curled and I was fighting myself, I could tell. It never worked if I fought myself.

Father blinked the sleep out of his eyes and put his hands on my shoulders, reassuringly. He had enormous hands that could crush me if they wanted, but he was always gentle.

"Rob—rob—ers." I pointed at the door, and Father's eyes widened.

"In the house?" he whispered.

I pointed to my ear and nodded. Father shot his attention toward the door. The wood looked thin. He passed me the oil lamp and threw the pillow off his bed. Beneath was an ornate oak box.

An ivory-handled revolver was cushioned inside, a gift from some nobleman. Father brandished the gun and pushed open the bedroom door.

When we got to Tim's room, he was still asleep. It's nearly impossible to wake him up without pulling him out of bed, so that's what Father did.

"Huh! What's it?" Tim gasped as he hit the floorboards. He spotted me first. "Marlin! I'll kill you, you peeve!"

Father knelt and put a hand over Tim's mouth.

"Marlin's heard intruders," he whispered.

"Sure it's not voices in your head?" Tim said, pushing Father's hand away.

"Quiet."

"I was quiet before you barged in," Tim mumbled.

Father glared at him, and Tim cast down his eyes. He'd forgotten who he was talking to. Father pushed us both behind him, and the three of us made our way into the hall. Father kept the pistol close to his side and told me to hold the lamp high. We descended the stairs and checked the dining room. It was empty. Then the parlor and the kitchen. No one was there.

I felt a pinch at my back. "Ah!" I cried.

Father spun on me with the gun. The Jungle Look flashed for a moment, and I thought he'd shoot me. Then he lowered the gun.

"Silence," he slowly mouthed. Behind me, Tim was trying to hold his chuckling back.

We checked the library, the back way, the sunroom, the washrooms, and the closets. Father tested the bolts on the front and back doors. Both were engaged and undamaged.

"No signs," he said with a sigh.

"I'd hoped there were thieves," laughed Tim. "Then we could hand them Monkey Talker here as a hostage."

Father just looked tired. Tim laughed some more.

"Th-th-th—" I stuttered.

"I think we've had enough excitement for the night,"

Father said. "Let's go back to bed."

"That's it?" Tim said. "That's all he gets for waking us up in the middle of the night, with a new load of guests just arrived, to chase his imaginary friends?"

Father considered it for a minute. Then he held out his hand. "I'm sorry, Marlin."

"N-nnn-NNN—" *No*, I tried to say.

But he just looked at me with tired eyes.

I put my hand over my breast pocket, shivering slightly.

"Never more than a day." Tim shook his head in mock sympathy.

Father pushed my hand away and pulled the Paw out of my breast pocket. He passed it to Tim, who crowed triumphantly.

"Next time you have a nightmare," Tim whispered to me, "just wet your bed."

8.

Then the voices were back.

"They're gone."

"Let's move."

Tim and Father were definitely asleep again, and they'd crucify me if I woke them up. But there was someone in the house, I was sure of it.

I tried staying still, but I was shaking. There was a creak.

I turned the spark stone in Father's oil lamp, which he'd let me keep for the night, and stepped into the hall. If I could surprise them and start a commotion, maybe they'd be scared off. Or if they weren't, I could be loud enough to get Father out with his gun. I turned the flame to full burning and headed to the stairway.

"I'm afraid he hasn't got it."

The voice was above my head. *The attic. Of course,* I thought, *the one place we didn't look.* It was dark with lots of crates and junk everywhere, a good place to hide. I turned down the knob on the lamp until the flame was just a flicker and opened up the broom closet. My tiny light caught on the string that dangled from the attic trap door. I pulled it, and the wooden ladder slid down toward me. The voices grew louder.

"You have it?"

"Beautiful!"

It was shocking to hear them so close, but they sounded strangely small. I popped my head above the attic floor and saw movement by some crates in the corner. I pulled myself up and crept along the planks.

I glanced back toward the trap door. The only plan I really had was to pounce on them, turn up the light, then race back to the attic door and shove it closed behind me. I could prop it shut with a broom and call for Father.

"The big man's not so scary!" one voice chittered.

"Never said I was scared!" squealed another.

"He's old and slow!" They laughed.

I stood by the edge of the crates, steeling myself.

I am a Rackham, I thought, *and this is my home. I am my father's son.*

"Hah!" I leaped from the shadows and turned my lamp to full blast. Light chased darkness from the corner, and the shadows raced away.

"No!" one shrieked.

"The boy!" cried another.

51

"Run!" called a third.

All that remained was a half-eaten sausage torn apart on the floor. Little bites were missing, tiny, as if they'd been picked by a fingernail.

The thieves had been a circle of mice.

9.

I stumbled out into the night with my lamp in my hand and clambered down the hill in utter shock. The mud squished between my toes until I reached the Golden Path. And there, at the base of the pyramid, I could see all the torches that burned along the borders of the resort. Guards were posted at various points along the wall, but they all looked outward into the jungle. I quietly climbed the path to the cages.

I pressed my stomach to the fence of the Boar Den and looked in. Tuskus lay sleeping in the mud with Belly Wart by his side. Gray Beard was off in the corner. She opened her eyes and snorted at me.

"Hello, Marlin. Do you have some food?"

I pulled back the lamp and stood straight. Gray Beard's grunting woke up the other two pigs. Tuskus sniffed grumpily.

"Be quiet. I'm sleeping."

Gray Beard trotted to the fence, "Have you, Marlin?" she whined. I backed away and turned up the Path.

"What's the matter? What's the matter?" a pair of cockatoos called from their cage.

"It's Marlin! Wake up!" one of our bush dogs barked.

"What's going on out there?" moaned the spectacled bear.

I shook my head and slapped my face. I tried to tell myself I was in a dream, but my own voice was drowned out by the terrible noise of the zoo. Each caged animal I passed as I climbed up the pyramid snorted, bayed, growled, or hooted at me.

"Marlin! Marlin! Marlin!"

Surely this would bring the guards, and I'd look as crazy to them as I felt. So without thinking I called out to the animals. "Quiet!"

But it wasn't my voice, or at least not my language. I tried saying something else. "You'll wake everyone up!" I grunted and hissed. There were no words in what I said, not ones I could recognize, but the meaning was there.

A shout came from below me, one I couldn't understand. It was Zargo Hunt, a guardsman calling out something in his native tongue. He was coming up the pyramid toward me. I extinguished the light and ran.

The Monkey Maze was our largest exhibit by far. It took up nearly one entire side of the pyramid, and the Golden

Path cut through it via a caged pedestrian walkway. I tried to make my escape through there, but something caught my leg and I fell. I looked down to see a hairy hand holding me through the bars.

Another hairy hand grabbed my thigh. The first one left my foot, disappeared between the bars, and reemerged to take my shoulder. This hand pulled me up to my feet with surprising strength.

I followed the hairy hand down its arm to the other end and saw Trébone the orangutan staring at me.

"Did I hear you right?" he whispered.

I tried to knock his hand away, but the grip was too tight.

"You spoke!" he said in amazement. "How is this?"

I pushed back against the bars, trying to free myself. "I should be asking you!" I shouted.

Trébone shrieked and snaked his other arm through the bars to hold me. "What is this?" he gasped.

He stuck his thumb into my mouth and stretched out my cheek to look inside.

"Get your fingers out of my mouth!" I mumbled.

He reared back and laughed heartily. A few chimps and another orangutan padded over to the walkway.

"What you doing with him?" asked Screecher.

"Got some fruities for us, Marlin?" called Blue Boy.

"Get away, you fool!" Trébone slapped Blue Boy, and the chimp screeched at him.

The rest of the clan had woken up and were descending on us. They leaped up onto the bars and climbed to the iron roof of the walkway.

"Give us some beetles, Marlin!"

"I want nuts!"

"Fruities, Marlin, fruities!"

They were hooting and hollering, and their voices mushed together so much, I couldn't understand them. Just the howling noise of the monkey clan again, like I'd always heard from them.

"Shut your stupid mouths!" Trébone bellowed. "I cannot hear this boy speak!"

Blue Boy laughed. "A talking boy, Trébone?"

"Yes!" the orang shouted back. "Quiet your yap and you'll hear."

"Marlin, can you understand this?" Blue Boy stuck his thumb into his mouth and blew a raspberry at me.

"I have something for you!" called a chimp above my head, and I narrowly dodged a plop of something headed straight for my face.

Hysterical apes shook the cage bars with their laughter. Trébone was fixed on me.

"This is that jaguar they captured." He held me by the ears. "I have heard of jaguar magic."

The blood was rushing to my face, and Trébone's dirty thumbs were whirling around in my ear canals.

"Shut up in there!" someone shouted, in English this

time. Zargo was near. If he saw me, he would tell my father I was out at night.

"I've got to go." I pulled Trébone's fingers off my ears.

"To the jaguar's den," he said. "That is where you must go."

"Shut up!" Zargo shouted again. I broke free of Trébone's arms and ran out of the Monkey Maze.

"Jaguar food!" all the chimps called after me. "Jaguar food!"

10.

Before building the circus tent in the Sky Shrine, Father's pet project had been restoring the Ruby Palace. No one knows what it was used for in the old times, but it must have been important. All along the floors, walls, and ceiling were indentations the size of almonds. They were settings for precious stones, though the gems themselves were gone, stolen ages ago. Father couldn't afford to set all new gemstones there, but he wanted to reclaim the chamber's former glory, so he had all the indentations filled with chips of colored glass. They were red and blue and yellow, but at dusk, when the sun came straight through the entryway, the whole chamber lit up like a flame, and so he called it the Ruby Palace.

It sat empty for some time after it was restored, waiting for an animal that could live up to its majesty. The jaguar was a perfect fit.

The lock on the door hadn't been changed yet, so my skeleton key still opened it. I entered the chamber in darkness and sat in silence with whatever was on the other side of the bars. It took me some time to raise the courage to relight my lamp.

I turned the spark stone, and the wick caught flame. The glow of the light reflected in the hundreds of colored glass chips embedded in the walls, floor, and ceiling. It was like being inside the eye of a dragonfly. A red halo grew around the stones on the other side of the bars, but it didn't touch the jaguar; he was still a shadow. I turned the knob of the lamp, feeding more oil to the wick, and the glow intensified in the hundreds of facets. But the jaguar stayed an inky nothing.

Then he opened his eyes. They were a brighter yellow than the jeweled glass, and they considered me coolly, with that bored intelligence all cats seem to have. He didn't appear menacing, and I found myself drawn to him.

"Jaguar," I began. "What have you done to me?"

He appeared uninterested. His long body was stretched out over the floor of his cage, and his massive head rested on a paw. He blinked.

"Jaguar," I said again. "What did you do?"

His stare was blank. I began to feel foolish for talking to an animal and expecting an answer.

I hadn't been sleeping well lately. Perhaps that was the explanation. Was I sleepwalking?

The stones felt hard, and the bars of the jaguar's cage felt cold when I touched them.

"Am I dreaming?" I asked.

I crouched to the floor until my face was level with his. I looked into his yellow eyes.

"You must be asleep to dream," the jaguar said.

I jerked backward and fell on my wrist. A sharp pain pierced my hand, and when I pulled it out from under me, I saw I'd slashed myself, wrist to palm, on a broken shard of colored glass sticking up from the floor. I eyeballed the jaguar and put my bleeding hand to my lips.

"Does it taste like a dream?" the jaguar asked, purring.

I cradled the wound to my mouth and sucked. The blood was dripping down my chin and shirt. The jaguar flashed his eyes and raised his head.

"You should let me heal that for you." He stood up and stretched. "I have magic, if you couldn't already tell."

With that he let out an awful laugh, the muscles of his back tightened across his body, and his toes and jaw spread with power. *Magic,* I thought, *is that what this is?* I'd heard stories from the natives about the jungle and its strange inhabitants, but Father said it was fanciful thinking, something to amuse our guests but nothing to take seriously.

Yet here I was, talking to one of them.

My wrist was bleeding profusely now, and I unbuttoned my shirt and wrapped it around my arm. It soon soaked through with blood, and I felt myself becoming light-headed. No one knew where I was. If I fainted here, I might not wake up.

"Do you not believe me?" the jaguar asked, amused. "That cut is bad. This cave is sharp."

I could run back to the worker barracks and wake up Charro, our healer. Father had fired our proper doctor last month and hadn't found a replacement. Charro could handle a cut, though; I knew that.

But there would be questions. Why had I left the house at night? What was I doing in the Ruby Palace? After my complaints about the robbers, Father would think I'd gone mad.

"Give me the hand," the jaguar commanded. "Are you afraid of a captive like me?"

"You're a man-eater," I said. My hand was crying in pain.

"Where did you hear something like that?" the jaguar purred.

"Don't lie," I whispered. "You killed Nathtam, one of our men, when he was out in the jungle."

The jaguar considered this for a moment.

"I do not remember eating a man," he said. "Besides, I find your scent disagreeable."

"How'd he end up half eaten and hung from a tree?"

"I don't know. Perhaps he climbed it for fun but got so hungry on the way down, he ate himself." The jaguar laughed at his morbid joke.

"The workers say that jaguars are tricksters."

"That we are," cooed the jaguar. "Do you think this is a trick?"

I did, but my shirt was now completely soaked through, and the walls had begun to bend.

"Don't make me your enemy, as your father has," the jaguar said. "You will like me much more as a friend."

"What's your name?" I asked.

"My name?" He snorted. "Names are for men and their pets. I have my toes, my tongue, and my teeth. That's all the name I need."

"All the animals here have names, and you're one of them now," I said. "How can we be friends if I don't know your name?"

"Well, in that case you may call me Jaguar," he said. "I see no other jaguars here. If there were, I'm afraid I would be free and you would be dead."

I pulled my hand to my chest.

"Joking, only joking," the Jaguar purred. "Now, give it over."

The lightness in my head made it much easier to put my hand through the cage. I didn't feel any fear.

"This may sting," the Jaguar said, and he licked me.

His long tongue was like sandpaper, and it felt like he was lapping the skin right off my hand. A burning sensation spread from my palm to my shoulder and forced my hand away from him. I crumpled to the floor and rolled on the stone to try to put out the heat, but there were no flames.

62

The glowing lights of the Ruby Palace blurred together. I could hear the Jaguar choking and gagging and hacking something horrible.

Then my arm went cool. The room came into focus and the sweat on my forehead felt cold.

The Jaguar gasped for air. His black-as-night coat lightened to a charcoal gray, and he foamed at the mouth.

I turned over my hand and was shocked. The gash was gone, the skin unbroken. But more than that, the lines on the palm of my hand were missing. I closed it and watched them form, as if for the first time. It was new skin, untanned, untouched, unblemished, like a baby's. I felt a gentle throbbing in the soft flesh, as though a quiet power was resting there.

The Jaguar looked terrible. His face was drawn and thin, he shook on unsure legs.

"Some strange magic . . . ," I said.

"That's enough," the Jaguar heaved, "for tonight."

"My hand," I said. "You healed it!"

"Want me to bite it off?" the Jaguar barked. He coughed and retched at something in his throat.

"Enough," he growled. His eyes were glassy and terrifying. The moons had become as narrow as slits.

"G-good night, Jaguar," I said, grabbing the lamp from its hook. I backed my way out of the Ruby Palace, and a moan rose up behind me as I crept down the Golden Path.

All along my way, the animals were awake, but now they

stared at me silently. In awe or in fear, I don't know.

Back at the house, I hunkered into bed but was unable to sleep until I stuffed cotton in my ears to muffle the endless bickering of the mice.

SECOND DAY

Long night, eh? Perhaps the unusual sounds of the jungle made sleep difficult to come by? We know just what you need to recover: a catered breakfast in bed.

After boating up a winding river, touring the finest zoo in the world, and two-stepping your way through one of high society's most exclusive occasions, what could be better than mountains of fried eggs, boxcars of sausages, and oceans of juice and coffee?

You've earned it!

This is your time to relax and take in the brand-new world around you. The zoo and gardens are always open, and they are pulsing with life. There are eighty-seven different species of animals in our collection—you didn't think you could see them all in one day, did you?

Our staff is always hard at work caring for and feeding our many animals. Most of our collection are herbivores and eat fruits gathered by yet-to-be-civilized Tribesmen living in the jungle and delivered to our gates daily.

But for the carnivores in our zoo, fresh meat always comes in the form of a live feeding, just as it would in the wild. Bait animals are caught in the jungle or raised in the zoo, and for the bigger creatures in our care, mealtime proves to be quite a show.

Ask a friendly zoo hand about feeding times—but only if you've got the stomach for it!

II.

I t was the monkey fingers in my nose that woke me up.
"Pah!"

I opened my mouth to breathe and spotted Kenji sitting on my chest. Her tail was curled round her legs, and her arms were stretched out toward me, her fingertips disappearing into my nose. I shook my head and swatted at her. She flipped backward onto my belly and then crawled back up my chest. She screeched at me, but not in a language I could understand.

Disappointed, but a little relieved, I thought maybe it had been a dream.

Then I remembered to pull the cotton from my ears.

"—and Blue Boy said, 'Oh yes, he did. I heard it!'" Kenji went on, "but Kenji doesn't believe him because that stinky old chimp always lies to Kenji. But then it was Trébone who said, 'Oh yes, it's true!' and Kenji always listens to Trébone—"

Kenji was yapping at me, jumping up and down on my chest and tugging her mustache.

"—but Kenji had to know, so Kenji came here to wake you up, Master Marlin! So you can tell Kenji!"

Her little hands were gripping my eyebrows, and her mouth was less than an inch from my face.

I broke out laughing.

"Ahh!" Kenji howled. "It's true! You're a talking boy, Master Marlin!"

Kenji hopped off my chest and launched herself onto the bookshelf at the opposite wall. She scaled it and leaped like a furry cannonball onto my stomach.

"Ow!" I laughed, grabbing her by the scruff of the neck.

"This is crazy!" Kenji shouted happily.

"I know it is!"

"Kenji always thought you were so dumb, Master Marlin!"

"What?"

She laughed and tugged at her mustache. "Kenji's sorry, but it's true!"

"Well, I thought you were dumb," I said back.

Kenji froze. She pulled her mustache down past her shoulders.

"That does not make any sense." She cocked her head. "Why would Kenji be dumb?"

"Erm, I guess it doesn't?" I said, trying to make her feel better. "You're probably the smartest monkey I know."

Her face lit up. "Okay! You're the smartest person Kenji knows, too, Master Marlin!"

Kenji was my oldest friend. As strange and disarming as hearing an animal talk still was for me, I realized I'd been talking to them all for years, especially Kenji, and it was second nature to me. This felt even more natural than before.

"So you talked to the jaguar, Master Marlin?"

"Yeah, it was unbelievable," I said. "He told me he did this with magic. And then I cut my hand, and he healed it!" I showed Kenji the fair, untouched skin on my palm. It still felt raw and pulsing with energy.

"This isn't good, Master Marlin." Kenji said, backing away from it. "Magic is dangerous. Once it gets in you, you can't get it out."

"I don't know if I want it out," I said, marveling at my hand. "This is amazing. We're talking, but I don't even know how I'm doing it."

I tried to pay attention to the actual sounds I was making. Stutterers have to pay very close attention to sounds—they can be tricky things. Talking to Kenji now, I recognized that I wasn't speaking English and neither was she. But I wasn't hooting either, or screeching or howling like she was. I tried to say something to Kenji while focusing entirely on the sounds my mouth was making.

"Kk-kkk—Kooo—" I stuttered.

A disturbing development.

"What did you say?" Kenji looked confused.

 69

"I really don't understand this, Kenj," I said, trying not to overthink it. "When I speak to you, you understand what I say?"

"Uh . . . yeah, Master Marlin! What have we just been talking about?"

"I mean the sounds, Kenj." I sat up. "I know I'm not making the same sounds as you. You're a monkey making monkey sounds. Tuskus is a boar who makes boar sounds, and the Jaguar makes jaguar sounds."

"Yes." Kenji looked at me skeptically. "That is good. You figured that out."

"I know I'm stating the obvious," I said. "But how can all these different animals, who make all these different sounds, be understandable to me now? And how can you all understand each other?"

Kenji squinted her eyes and stroked her mustache thoughtfully. After a pause, she offered, "Kenji doesn't know. How come humans can't understand what anybody says?"

I leaned back on the bed. Maybe that was the better question.

It was time to take this new power on a test run. I asked Kenji to come with me on my chores around the zoo and help me get reacquainted with our animals.

Our first stop was the Blue Birdcage, an enclosure eleven yards high and about four times as wide. Three sides were made of thin bars that made viewing the birds easier, and there was a sturdy brick wall at the back.

The Blue Birdcage is one of my favorite parts of the zoo. Our resident storyteller and artist, Heppa, painted an enormous mural across the wall. It is a jungle scene, complete with vines, trees, shrubs, fallen logs, flowers, and insects all crowding one another. But the twenty or so birds that call it home tend to add their own kind of paint to the mural, so Kenji and I went in with a mop.

As soon as I closed the door behind me, our two rainbow toucans, Eddo and Bill, flew down from their ropes hanging overhead.

"Ah! It's him!" Bill said to Eddo.

"The boy-who-talks-to-jaguars!" Eddo said to Bill.

"How exciting!" they both said together. Each cocked his head side to side, looking at me expectantly.

I felt nervous and turned to Kenji. "What do you say to a toucan?" I asked her.

"Say good morning!" Kenji threw up her arms and turned to Eddo and Bill. "He's just learned how to talk yesterday, so you gotta give him a little time."

"I didn't just learn how to talk yesterday," I said, annoyed. "I just learned to talk *to animals* yesterday!"

"So who were you talking to before?" Eddo asked.

"Other people," I said, but then thought about it. "Well, no, I didn't really do much of that either."

"Like I said," Kenji went on. "Yesterday."

"Well, that's just wonderful," Bill squawked.

"Yes, excellent." Eddo echoed.

"Look-it! Look-it! Look-it!" a little bird called from the corner of the cage. It was Tappet, our new bird of paradise. He was prancing violently about and making an awful racket.

"I despise that creature." Bill flapped his colored wings angrily.

"Hate him!" Eddo cawed.

"Yeah," I said to the toucans. "What's his problem?"

"He doesn't have a problem," said Bill.

"We're the ones with the problem," said Eddo.

"We've got to listen to him," they said together.

Over in the corner, Tappet was gyrating and vibrating and making a terrible noise. He'd buried his face in his chest and stuck his wings straight out in the shape of a T. There was one brilliant blue dot on each wing, so he looked like a face with two giant eyes.

I knew from watching other birds of paradise with my father that this was a mating dance. But even though there were two girl birds of paradise in the enclosure, he never paid attention to either of them. He'd been dancing and cawing like a madman ever since he arrived.

Kenji and I looked at each other and nodded.

"What are you doing there, Tappet?" I asked, walking over.

The bird flipped his head off his chest and peered at me.

"Oh, Marlin." He considered me for a moment. "So it's true what I heard about you and the jaguar. And now here you are, talking like a regular bird. Very impressive, I say!"

With that he buried his beak back in his feathers, popped out his wings, and resumed the dance. "Look-it! Look-it! Look-it!"

"Kenji isn't too fond of this bird, Master Marlin!" Kenji said, plugging her ears.

I approached him, saying, "Tappet, why are you still—"

"Back it up! Back it up!" He fiercely pecked the air to keep me from his circle. "This is my spot!"

"I'm sorry," I said stepping back. "But can I talk to you for just one minute?"

He was still.

"Why do you go on like this?"

"Why do I dance?" He puffed up his chest and raised his little birdy chin. "I dance for love."

"He's trying to mate with a bird, Master Marlin," said Kenji. "You know what that is?"

"Yes, Kenji, I work in a zoo," I whispered. "But which bird is he going for? If she's not interested, maybe we could move her to another cage."

"Which bird?" Tappet cried, overhearing me. "Why, you crazy boy. Is your taste so unrefined?"

"I suppose it is," I said.

"You are standing before her and still cannot see." Tappet laughed. "Did the jaguar trade you speech for your sight?"

I cast my eyes around the cage, but the two female birds of paradise were all the way on the other side. "Tappet, who are you talking about?"

"It's her," Kenji said, pointing at the wall. "But she doesn't say anything."

"Look-it! Look-it! Look-it!" Tappet turned away from me and went back to his dance.

He was chirping at the wall.

"There's no bird there," I said.

"You don't see?" Kenji pointed. "The little brown bird in the grass."

She was pointing to the mural on the wall. In the mess of painted leaves and grass, there was a small brown figure. A female bird of paradise.

"Oh, Kenji," I said. "That's just a painting." I leaned forward and put my hand on the painted bird.

"Keep your hands off her, you knave!" Tappet leaped into the air and thrust his beak at me. I jerked back my hand and retreated with Kenji.

"And don't you come back!" Tappet howled.

I told Kenji to wait outside the Arts and Leisure Building.

"But how can she be so flat like that?" she shrieked. "Kenji has never seen a flat bird!"

"Because she's not a bird," I said for the third or fourth time as I walked into the building.

"Looks like a bird to Kenji."

"That's our problem," I whispered to myself.

Jarro was at the front desk, which meant that his mother, Heppa, was teaching a class. That meant I couldn't sneak in unnoticed and get what I needed.

"Young Rackham," Jarro said when he saw me. "Good day to you. Can I do something for you?"

I nodded and prepared myself to speak, thinking of how I could get my message across in the fewest words possible.

"Ta-TA-taaaaahh—kk." *Talk,* I managed to say with great effort, and I think Jarro understood me. I decided to skip the connecting words of the phrase and just get to the subject. "HH—Hhhheeee—Hhhhehhh-ehhh. . ."

"Talk to Heppa?" Jarro said for me. "You want to talk to my mother?"

He put a slight emphasis on the word *talk* and couldn't help smiling. The employees' disrespect was nothing new, but I could never get over the shame.

He gestured to a mahogany door across the hall, and I shuffled toward it. I cracked it open and peeked through.

"A color is not like a bachelor, eating dinner alone at home," Heppa said in her heavy Arawak accent. "He has a brother somewhere, a sister, parents, a wife! If he gets lucky, he might even have some children appear at his table." Heppa spotted me peeking through the door and discreetly waved me in. "There is a family in your colors, and each relationship is unique. Green and blue have not spoken for several years. Yellow and red are in business together; purple and orange are having a baby." Heppa put a hand to the side of her mouth. "But it is an ugly baby."

A large table full of female guests tittered at Heppa's joke. They wore paint-covered smocks over their fancy vacation wear and worked on nature scenes.

Heppa stepped away from the table and led me to the back of the classroom. "Hello, my dear." She greeted me warmly and wrapped leathery arms around my neck. Her embrace was comforting; she was like the grandmothers I'd read about in books.

I felt unsure of myself from my encounter with Jarro and took a deep breath in anticipation of speaking, but Heppa gave me a look of infinite patience.

"Heppa!" a lady in a red hat called out. "Can you help me, please?"

"In a moment, darling," Heppa said sweetly. "I am conversing with my friend."

She turned back to me and I very simply said, "P-paint?"

"Of course." She smiled and led me to a cart full of supplies. "Take anything you wish."

"Seeds! Seeds!"

Kenji made an excellent distraction, dragging an open bag of seeds around the Blue Birdcage. All the birds jumped off their perches and madly chased her. Even Tappet, deciding his dance could wait, left his girlfriend on the wall and went to get some breakfast.

Amidst the chaos, I rushed over to the corner where the painted brown bird was. I thought it'd be cruel to paint her off the wall entirely; Tappet would be heartbroken, wondering where she'd gone. So I decided on a different plan.

Female birds of paradise are drab creatures, usually just two shades of brown. But males, like Tappet, are brightly colored, with beaks and wings in yellows, greens, and blues. So I took my paints and made some colorful embellishments.

Once the seeds had run out and the birds stopped chasing Kenji round the cage, Tappet returned to his little clearing by the mural. Kenji and I watched from the farthest wall as he cleaned up his display area, stretched out his wings, and prepared to dance. He squawked once, and froze.

He hopped up close to the wall and leaped backward, then leaned toward it again.

"I'm sorry, my friend," he said to the mural. "I suppose that's my mistake."

He laughed, shook himself off, and flew up into the ropes, where the two real birds of paradise were waiting.

12.

Having the power of animal speech made me infinitely better at my job. I solved problems that had been plaguing us for months. After cleaning up the Blue Birdcage, I learned that the bats were getting sick because their berries weren't ripe, and I made a note to replace them out. Dreyfus hadn't been drinking enough water because someone had raised a flagpole by his water trough and it was scaring him. The sloths told me they'd feel safer if there were more branches on the fake trees, and I gladly installed some. The tapirs had me dig them a mud bath so they could keep from getting sunburned. But the greatest victory of the day was helping Mala, our spectacled bear.

Mala hadn't been nursing her little cub, Bashtee, so I had to enter the den a few times a day to feed him donkey milk from a bottle. This was bad for two reasons. The first is that babies need what's in their mother's milk to stay healthy. The second is that to get donkey milk, you have to milk a donkey, and I'm not even going to tell you what that's like.

When I asked Mala why she hadn't been nursing her cub, she told me that he'd gone missing after she birthed him. "That's the boy's cub," Mala said. "Not mine."

"This is Bashtee," I said, astonished. "He's yours. I watched it happen."

Mala shook her head and turned away from me.

Kenji whispered, "The cub doesn't have the right smell. That's why she thinks it's not hers."

Bashtee was in my arms, sucking a bottle of milk.

"Why don't you smell right?" I asked him.

"Because of Master Marlin's brother!" Kenji said, grabbing my ear. "Kenji saw him take the cub out of the cage."

Tim knows not to touch newborn mammals. Father lectures us every time one is born. Mothers sometimes abandon their cubs if we touch them when they're too young.

"Why would he do that?" I asked Kenji.

"There was a tall girl with him," Kenji said.

That was all I needed to know.

So Tim's scent on the cub prevented his mother from recognizing him, and now the workers and I were in there bottle-feeding him five times a day and making it worse.

"This is your cub!" I told Mala. But she only sulked in the corner of the cage.

If I'd learned one thing from Tappet that morning, it was

that animals saw things differently than I did. If I wanted to live with them and help them, I'd have to look at the world from their point of view.

I told Kenji to fetch me a big fluffy towel from the bath house and meet me at the river. I had nearly finished washing Bashtee when Kenji arrived. Then I rolled him in mud and picked him up with the towel, careful not to make contact with my skin. Finally, I dropped Bashtee in a bucket of dung from Mala's den. Not the most civilized solution, but it was the best I could think of.

After he was good and covered, I picked him up with the towel and carried him back to the Bear Den. I slipped him through the door of the cage when Mala wasn't looking and snuck off with Kenji.

We sat for nearly half an hour on the roof of the Butterfly House with a pair of binoculars. Mala finally padded across the length of cage and sniffed Bashtee. The mother bear hesitated for a moment, twitched her ears, and then relaxed her body and rolled over.

Bashtee climbed onto his mother's tummy and started to nurse.

There was one place in the zoo Kenji wouldn't go: the Snake House.

It was a big sturdy building down near the base of the pyramid. Its walls were made of stone and its roof was wood and tar, but we thatched it with leaves for a rustic feel. It was kept dark for the comfort of the animals, but it created a rather frightening environment for the guests.

It was Dead Eyes that scared them.

Inside the Snake House, we had species ranging from four inches all the way up to six and a half feet, but Dead Eyes was the star of the show. We kept him behind a wide panel of triple-thick glass. His exhibit was dim, and he rarely moved. On tours, Father would stop at his display and ask guests what they saw. They'd point out rocks, mounds of dirt, and logs. Then Father would reveal that every bump and texture and curve and rise that they thought was decoration was really thirty feet and eleven hundred pounds of giant anaconda.

Dead Eyes was already blind when Father found him, but he often snapped at the guests through the glass. He'd slam his head into the barrier and hiss. Nothing would get through the triple-thick glass, but it scared people so badly that Father laid rugs on the floor to muffle vibrations. This day, though, Dead Eyes was unusually still.

It was late afternoon, and Kenji had gone off to brighter quarters of the zoo. I decided I didn't need her help to talk with the animals, so I just walked up to a tank of iguanas and said hello. They didn't respond, so I opened the lid of their tank a crack in case they couldn't hear me.

"Hello there!" I said again.

They didn't respond, and neither did the other lizards, or any of the snakes. Perhaps they didn't understand me for some reason, or perhaps they didn't care.

With no one to talk to, I thought it'd be a good idea to check the worksheet. I unlocked the staff room in back and closed the door behind me.

Each species of snake prefers certain foods at specific times, with different intervals between meals. Some eat every few hours, and some get sick if they're fed more than once a week. Everyone on the chart looked up-to-date except Dead Eyes, who was due for an afternoon meal.

I turned to the small pen in the corner of the staff room. We keep the young capybaras meant for Dead Eyes there. A capybara is a very large rodent that lives in the jungle, something like a giant guinea pig. They weigh about three hundred thirty pounds when they're full-grown, but the ones we keep for snake food never grow that large. They're hardly teenagers when Dead Eyes gets them.

"Hello," a furry-snouted creature chirped at me. "Do you know where my brother has gone?"

For the first time, this new power didn't seem so great.

In the pen, there were five little piles of straw where each of the five young capybaras had been growing up. They were born a few weeks previously to Bucktooth, one of the females of the Capybara Camp in the zoo proper. Father decided we had enough capys on display and sent these babies to be used as snake food.

This capy was the only one left.

"I haven't seen my brother in a few days," the small

creature mewed. "Before that my other brother left, and before that my sisters."

I felt a little ill.

"Do you know where they've gone?"

"Um, hello," I said, blanching.

"Hello," he said in a friendly tone.

I checked the feeding schedule again. DEAD EYES: ONE (1) CAPYBARA. And the date was today. This fellow was on the schedule.

"Can you help me find them?" he asked.

I'd fed one animal to another before. I'd done it countless times. I'd eaten animals myself: deer, fish, snakes, frogs. Though I suppose they weren't alive when I ate them. And they certainly weren't speaking to me.

"It's getting lonely in here."

I didn't know what to do. Dead Eyes had to eat. We'd put him in a cage. He couldn't hunt. That meant we had to feed him.

As long as he was in that cage, I had to feed him little capybaras or else he'd die.

"I . . . I don't want to lie to you," I said to the little creature.

"Don't want to lie to me about what?" he asked.

My lunch felt unsettled in my stomach. I believe I'd had venison that day.

"I know where your brothers and sisters are."

"You do?" he chirped.

"It's not good news," I said. "They've been eaten. By a snake."

The capybara's hair stood up all over his body. His eyes grew wide. His lips pulled back.

"Is there a snake here? I thought I smelled something bad."

He lifted his forepaws to the edge of the pen and tried to jump out, but it was too high.

"Please save me!" he begged. "Please save me from the snake!"

He was scared but gave me a trusting look. He didn't know I was here to make a meal of him. That I'd done it before, even taken one of his brothers when the group was sleeping and dropped him in with Dead Eyes. I'd hardly thought twice about it.

"Okay," I said finally. "I'll get you out of here."

One creature eats another, the circle of life—I knew all that. But I wasn't going to kill this little creature asking for my help. I'd sneak him out of the Snake House and take him outside the walls of the zoo, and work all that moral stuff out later.

"You will?" the capy said. "Oh, thank you!"

I nodded at him. All I'd need to do was somehow figure what Dead Eyes would eat.

"I know! I know! I'm late!" Leedo Flute burst into the staff room in a huff. "It's a very busy day—sometimes I get behind!"

He took the worksheet out of my hand and laid it on the table, then pushed past me and grabbed the capybara.

"I don't need a little boy doing my job for me all the time." He tucked the capy under his arm. "You trying to get me in trouble with your father?"

The capybara squealed, "Help!"

I tried to grab it out of Leedo's hands, but he swatted me away.

"What's the point talking to you anyway?" He pushed past me into the main room of the Snake House. "Leedo does his job—don't let anybody say different."

"SS—s—ST—ST-aaa-aaa—" I stuttered.

The whole day, I'd been completely fluent, but now I was a stutterer again, and my voice was useless. I had to catch him. But he was moving so fast that by the time I managed to get a hand on his belt, he was already at the feeding chute of Dead Eyes's display.

He turned around and looked at me.

"Yeah, Marlin? What is it?"

He opened the hatch and dropped the capybara down the chute. It closed with a metallic clang, and the creature slid down into the anaconda's chamber.

I pushed Leedo out of the way, opened the chute, and shot my hand down, trying to pull the little creature out. An earthquake of movement rose up against my hand and forced it out of the chute. The hatch slammed shut and Dead Eyes was still.

It was over.

I chose to neglect work for the rest of the day. At the dinner table that evening, I found myself unhappily presented with a plate of sliced duck.

I didn't touch it.

I couldn't even look.

SECOND NIGHT

We know this resort comes highly recommended. If you hadn't read the thrilling accounts and seen the etchings in the newspapers, you wouldn't have sailed all the way to the Edge of the World.

We know you had high expectations when you arrived.

But did you imagine that the jungle would be this beautiful? The picture books and travelogues pale in comparison to its wonder. Dark mysteries and unspeakable secrets are being revealed to you one by one.

Tonight, we invite you to gaze up at the stars and let your imagination soar through a guided tour of the night sky: the home of the Jungle Gods.

The native people of this land have long seen their guardians in the constellations. Join Heppa, our resident artist and storyteller, as she regales you with tales of the Old Times and the Gods That Dance in the Sky.

You may snicker to hear it, but many natives still believe these stories are true. And while we can't vouch for the tales' authenticity, be assured they are wonderful legends that may leave you thinking of them long after the telling is done.

13

"Before the people of your world came to this place, the Gods of the Night danced through the sky."

Heppa stood before an assembled crowd of guests and raised her arms. "When I was a small child, I saw them dance. I can still remember this."

I didn't attend Heppa's starlight routine much anymore. I'd heard all the stories a hundred times, but Father had tasked Tim and me, and a few workers, with moving animals in preparation for the circus the next day. We were to do it at midnight, so I had a few hours to kill.

I suppose I also may have been feeling reflective.

We were on the Great Lawn, with blankets and woven mats spread across the grass by the dozens. The guests were huddled in groups of families and friends. They had been given small telescopes to view the night sky, and servants were making their way from blanket to blanket handing out chilled milk with cocoa beans.

"They aren't dancing now!" a man with a long black mustache called out. The lady guest in the red hat from Heppa's painting class turned and scowled at him from where she sat, up front with the rest of the students from that afternoon.

"They did dance," Heppa intoned. "For those first few magical years of my life, I saw them dance. When the ships came, that's when they stopped."

The members of the painting class were entranced, and their enthusiasm slowly spread through the crowd. Heppa raised a wrinkled hand to the sky and traced a line connecting seven stars in a group.

"Slint, the rainbow bird," she said. "The mother of this place. Long ago, before anything was here but a great flooded plain, Slint flew across the sky and dropped a seed from another land. It fell in the floodplain and grew into the first tree. That tree multiplied and its family pushed back the flood until it was a single river. Slint dropped more seeds, for plants and animals and fish. In the night you can see Slint's egg." Here Heppa pointed to the moon. "Every thirty nights, Slint lays a new egg, and you can watch it hatch and give birth to something new."

"What's it give birth to?" asked the lady in the red hat.

"No one knows!" Heppa smiled. "It's too dark to see up there!"

The crowd broke into laughter. Heppa had them now, as she always did. She waited for the laughter to die down before snapping her fingers and pointing.

"Do you see him? Be quick! It's Alguna, the bloody hare."

She pointed to a small speck in the sky that I knew wasn't a star at all; it was Mars, and it changed its position in the sky throughout the year.

"Alguna races amongst the gods, one day here and one day there, always running for his life! See how his white fur has been stained with blood? That's because he's been clawed and bitten. In the time it takes for ten of Slint's eggs to hatch, Alguna will be attacked by Mirgas, the snake"— she traced a line of six stars—"Ruupt, the crocodile; and Banta, the eagle." She pointed them out to the crowd.

"He has not yet been caught, and his frantic run will never end. That is the way with things big and small. The strong may rest, but the weak must always run."

The capybara couldn't run.

"But," Heppa exclaimed, "Alguna is no fool! He stays far away from Kocaru."

She pointed to a grouping of stars set apart from the others. Three faint white dots made a tail, a group of five were the body, and two extraordinarily bright stars, almost yellow in their hue, were the eyes.

"Kocaru, the black jaguar. Eater of the sky!"

"All right, I want to keep this short and sweet." Tim considered me with contempt. "We're going to nab just three apes. Orangs or chimps, it doesn't matter. Rope them, lead them to the mobile, lock the door, and we're done. Simple enough?"

Zargo Hunt, Leedo Flute, Manray Lightfoot, and I all stood at attention. I was on the end, trying to avoid Leedo.

"Sound simple?" Tim barked at us.

"Yes, sir!" shouted the men. I sputtered nervously.

It was pretty normal for us to take animals out of their permanent cages and put them in mobile ones if they got sick or we had to transport them somewhere, but I'd never before been on a capture crew taking dangerous animals like apes out of their cages. I'm not sure why Father stuck me on this job when I could just as easily have been moving tapirs. Maybe he thought of me differently after I got the collar around the Jaguar. Whatever it was, I could tell Tim didn't like being stuck with me.

Zargo Hunt, the guard from the night before, smiled at me reassuringly. "You will do well, young Rackham."

"Thhh-TH-th-TH-aa-anks," I stuttered.

"Have something to say?" Tim sneered at me.

I shook my head no.

"Then listen to me," he snapped. "Chimps are dangerous. You want to get someone hurt?"

I lowered my head and shook it again.

Father wanted three apes in mobile carriers so we could wheel them up to the Sky Shrine for the next day's circus show. Tim signaled Zargo to unlock the gate of the Monkey Maze. Leedo was breathing heavily, and I noticed that my hand was shaking. The maze is home to three orangutans and thirty-seven chimpanzees. Father ordered a whole mess of them from Africa and Borneo, thinking most wouldn't survive the boat ride. They all did, and we were left with an almost unmanageable population. They starved out all the South American primates we lodged them with at the zoo, and Father was forced to construct this enormous exhibit just to handle them all.

We'd never tried to take any out before. It struck me as strange that we'd captured a man-eating jaguar, been visited by a duke who Father apparently hated, and were pulling chimpanzees out of the Monkey Maze all in the same week.

The key turned in the lock, and the gate swung open. I'd never actually been inside the maze proper before, just thrown food through the bars and let the apes sort for themselves who got to eat what.

We call it a maze for a reason. When Father had the enclosure built, he dumped topsoil and planted trees all through the Monkey Maze. It was like a miniature jungle in there, with trees and vines growing all the way up the iron bars that covered the top. Some branches pushed their way between the bars, and we had to prune them from the roof of the cage so they didn't bend openings with their growth.

Chimps knuckle-walked toward the forested area at the center as the five of us entered.

"Men coming in!" I heard one of them screech. There
was ape laughter in the trees. It was an awful sound.

"All right, men." Tim tried to keep his voice steady. "We move as a group and take one at a time."

"Yes, Mr. Rackham," Zargo said. Then he turned to Manray and said something in Arawak.

"No jungle talk," Tim chided.

"I was just relaying your order, sir," said Zargo.

"How will he ever learn the Queen's English?" Tim turned to Manray and pointed sharply at himself. "Listen to me. Follow me."

Leedo cast me an accusatory glance and huffed. As though Tim treated me any better!

"To the trees," Tim barked, and we followed him, though I didn't know what Tim's strategy was. The majority of the apes were in the treed area, but it seemed like we'd have better luck catching stragglers who were meandering around the clearings.

But we ended up under the trees.

"What are you doing here, Marlin?" a chimp called down to me from a hidden branch.

"Lot of men with you," said another. "Why do they have those catchers?"

Each of us was armed with a large wooden bar that had a wire lasso on the end, much like the one I'd used to collar the jaguar. I suppose we were meant to snare apes with them, but in the dark, under the trees, they seemed useless.

"Oh, Mr. Tim," Leedo said with a mix of irritation and fear. "We might have better luck catching monkeys in the clearing. Where, you know, we can see."

"Quiet!" Tim said. "You'll give us away." He crept between the trees, cautiously stepping over vines—believing, I guess, that the apes didn't know where he was.

"Walking pretty funny, that one is!" called down another chimp from a tree.

"Don't step on a flower!"

"Or trip!"

Blue Boy launched himself down from a branch and landed on Tim's back, toppling him over in the dirt. Manray stabbed his lasso at the ape, but Blue Boy jumped away, and Manray only managed to club Tim in the calf with the rod.

"Ow!" Tim yelped. "Grab him!"

Manray swiped again, but his lasso caught on a tree branch as Blue Boy scaled it, laughing to his friends, "Slow, aren't they?"

Tim refused Zargo's help and picked himself up. "What was that?" he shouted.

Manray looked to Zargo for a response, but Tim put up his hand. "I'm asking you," he said, pointing at Manray.

Manray blinked and pointed to the tree.

"I know he went into the tree," Tim fumed. "What I want to know is why you didn't catch him."

"Mr. Tim," Leedo said again. "This is a hard place to catch a monkey—let's try the clearing."

"Do you want to go where things are easy, Mr. Leedo," Tim mocked him, "or do you want to go where your job is?"

I heard a chittering in the trees.

"Ready to go?" one chimp said to another.

"That's what I thought," said Tim. "Now, form up behind me, and the next chimp that comes thro—"

A black mass dropped down behind Tim. Then more came down all around us. Zargo grunted and I saw him fall under the apes.

Then there were shouts, and my mouth was tasting the ground. All I could see was a small glint of moonlight in the dewy grass.

14.

"Your friends ran away, tiny man," a familiar voice said in my ear. "What are they doing, leaving you here by yourself?"

I raised my head and spit. There was gritty dirt on my teeth and gums. I felt a fuzzy hand on my neck and craned it to see Trébone, orange and black in the moonlight, smiling at me. Nearly a dozen chimps surrounded us.

"No melons today, Marlin?" one laughed.

"This doesn't look like sugarcane," said Screecher, picking up the rod and lasso. He tossed it over my head to another chimp, and they made a game of keeping it in the air above me.

"Each of us was snared with this," said Trébone, "and once is enough."

The chimpanzees shook with laughter, slapping their chests and hopping up and down.

"Maybe we catch you, huh?" Blue Boy snatched the rod from the air and lassoed me around the neck. He leaped over my back and pulled me up to my knees. "That how you do it?"

"Easy now," Trébone said, reaching to take the rod away.

Blue Boy slapped the orangutan's hand. "That's how they did me!"

I dug my fingers at my neck, trying to get between the wire and my skin. "Huuuhh!" I gasped for air. The chimps tittered. I felt my face swell with blood.

"That's enough," Trébone ordered. "Loosen it up!"

The folds of his face bunched up near his eyes, and he glared at Blue Boy.

The wire slacked and I could feel the blood in my head and chest reconnect.

"I was just playing with him," Blue Boy murmured. But he didn't remove the noose from my neck.

Trébone leaned close to me.

"I hear you went to the jaguar like I told you," he said. "Was he the one who made you talk?"

"He was," I said.

"That jaguar is funny." Screecher laughed heartily. "A boy who talks!"

"Too bad he can't make you smart!" said Blue Boy.

"We caught a talking boy!" Screecher hooted, and many of the apes joined in. "Let's make him do some tricks!"

"Did he tell you why?" Trébone asked, leaning closer and

whispering so the other apes couldn't hear.

"He didn't. But I fell and cut myself and he licked the cut and healed me." I held out the palm of my right hand, which was untanned and plump, the lines of a palm just starting to settle in.

Trébone leaped back. "That's powerful magic!" he cried out. The apes around him seemed surprised at his reaction, and he tried to compose himself.

"It feels weird," I said of the new skin. "Like, I can feel my heartbeat in it all the time. And it's a little warmer than my other hand."

"Very strange," Trébone mused. "I've heard of this but never seen it with my eyes."

"I've never even heard," said Blue Boy, who still had the noose around my neck. "And I say it's unnatural." Some apes murmured in agreement. "I say we kill him!"

Several more cheered. The noose jerked tighter.

"We do no such thing," Trébone growled to the crowd. "The jaguar chose this boy. We don't mess with one like him." The other apes shrank at the sound of his voice, but Blue Boy was unconvinced.

"Then what?" the chimp snarled. "He's in our home with catchers. You want this around your neck, Trébone?"

The orang considered for a moment. I sensed the crowd wavering between the two.

"I'm sorry I'm in your place," I spoke up. "I really didn't want to come here. It was my father who ordered us in."

"His father," Blue Boy said, "the catcher man."

"He's doing a special show tomorrow, in another part of the zoo. He wanted us to take three of you," I said, looking around at the angry faces. "We were just going to keep you in mobiles for the night, you know, those little cages that can move. It would be a quick show, the guests would look at you, and then we'd drop you off back here. No harm done. Maybe extra treats?"

"Well, it looks like the show's over." Trébone smiled. "We've chased your friends out."

"Now they see who's strongest." Blue Boy beat his chest, and the other chimps followed suit.

"Yes, I see that," I said very cautiously, "but I'm afraid they'll come back. And more of them."

"Then we'll fight again!" Blue Boy hollered.

The apes beat their chests and hooted.

"You won't be able to," I said. "They'll bring nets and guns and drag you away from here. They might kill you."

The chimps went quiet at that. They must have seen guns when they were captured in Africa.

"If you come with me," I said, taking a deep breath, "I can promise you won't get shot."

Blue Boy started to laugh, but Trébone raised his hand to him.

"I only need three of you," I went on. "We'll go out together. You'll spend the night in the mobiles, and I'll make sure you have extra food. But we have to go now, because they'll be coming soon with nets and guns."

Trébone looked around the circle at his apes. "Can we trust you, boy?" he asked, turning back to me.

"I give you my word."

That cracked him up. "Your word!" Trébone laughed.

I smiled awkwardly, and the chimps didn't look convinced.

"I swear to you," I said. "On my honor. You'll be safe."

"Men have no honor," Blue Boy said.

"But they have guns," Trébone answered. "They don't need honor."

With that he snatched the rod from Blue Boy's hand and lifted the noose up and away from my neck, then swung it around and latched it onto Blue Boy's wrist.

"What's this?" Blue Boy shouted.

Trébone picked a second rod off the ground and tightened the noose around his and Screecher's arms, binding them together.

"You said 'never trust a man,'" Blue Boy growled.

"I don't!" Trébone answered. "But this is just a boy, and one who can talk. And I don't know about you, but I don't want to get shot."

The orang turned to me and extended the rod. "We're in your hands, boy."

Father was at the gate of the Monkey Maze with Tim and a dozen men. They had nets and knives and rifles. They were here to rescue me.

Imagine their surprise when I walked out from the trees with two chimps and an orang in my lassos, all ambling behind me docilely.

The astonished looks on their faces told me that, for once, I didn't need words.

15

I entered the Ruby Palace that night and nearly screamed. The Jaguar was not in his cage.

Instead, I found him in the middle of the observation area, several feet in the air, as though in midleap.

I closed my eyes and prepared for the worst. But I felt nothing. He didn't devour me.

I saw a vertical glimmer in front of the Jaguar's face and turned up the oil flow in my lamp. The Ruby Palace was illuminated with its usual brilliance. And I saw that the Jaguar was in the middle of the room and several feet in the air, but not because he was pouncing on me. He stood there in a mobile carrier, a cage within a cage.

"Are you in the circus tomorrow?" I said, as much to myself as to the Jaguar.

"I never know my own fate anymore," the Jaguar said.

"You must be," I said. "That's why you're in the carrier.

Why didn't Father mention it?"

"He's not nearly as talkative with me as you are," the Jaguar said dryly.

"Didn't mention it to me, I mean." I pulled the Paw out of my pocket. "Look what he gave me."

The Jaguar eyed it stone-faced. "If I'd known you were such a fan of dead hands, I would have brought some for you."

"You don't understand," I said. "It's something between my brother and me. You get the Paw for doing something good."

"And you've done something good?" the Jaguar asked.

"Yeah," I said. "I got the monkeys to agree to be caged for the night. Otherwise Father would have had to go in with nets and guns. He said I'd probably saved a chimp's life."

"Ahh," the Jaguar purred. "So it's something good according to him."

"What do you mean?" I asked, offended.

The Jaguar only laughed.

"What's so special about this Paw? Is it enchanted?"

"No," I answered. "It just means you've done something clever or brave."

"So he saves all the good charms for himself."

"What are you talking about?" I said. "There are no enchantments here."

"Don't lie to me. I saw him throw open these bars like he was snapping a twig. I tried them in every spot, and they are unbreakable. What magic keeps me here?"

It surprised me to realize that, even with all his strange power, the Jaguar was still an animal.

"What is keeping you in there," I said, "is called a lock. And it isn't magic, it's a machine. Do you know what that is?"

The Jaguar thought for a moment.

"It's a curse?"

"A machine isn't magic," I repeated. "It's a thing. Something that people make out of . . . well, other things." I lifted my oil lamp in the air. "Like this, for example."

"Ah," said the Jaguar, "a piece of moonlight you've captured in a jar. Very clever."

"No." I said, "It isn't moonlight. It's an oil lamp. You see, we take the fat from a humpback whale,"—the Jaguar cocked his head—"which is a kind of . . . a giant fish, I suppose, that lives in the ocean. We take the fat from its body and smash it up and put it in a little clear jar like this one. And then we spin a special rock called flint that makes a spark, and it sets the whale fat on fire. And that's how we make the light!"

The Jaguar considered this. "You set a giant fish on fire with a rock?"

"Well, when you say it like that, it doesn't make much sense—"

"That's how you said it."

"That's how you made me say it," I exclaimed, "because

you don't know anything! But I assure you, that's how it works. It is a machine, not magic, and it is the same with that lock."

"Hmm . . . a giant fish." The Jaguar braced his paw against the door. "That explains the strength. His soul is in the lock, and he obeys the men that put him there."

"No, no." I said, "There isn't a whale in the lock. It's a different machine, one made of metal. That's a very pure form of stone."

"Hardest stone I've encountered." The Jaguar winced. "Nearly cracked my teeth."

"Well, you shouldn't bite it." I wrapped my hands round the bars. "This is the strongest stuff in the world."

The Jaguar froze. His eyes flickered to my hands.

"Aren't afraid I'll take off your fingers?"

I realized I was inches from his mouth. My hand twitched, but I forced it to stay.

"You had your chance last night," I said stiffly. "And you didn't take it."

"I wasn't nearly as hungry last night."

Slowly, I released my grip and drew my hand toward my chest. "I'm not afraid of you."

"Not with this lock between us," the Jaguar said. "If it's so strong, how come that little man can open it?"

"Well, there's a casing here," I said, gesturing to the lock, "and inside that is a metal latch. A latch is a kind of hook that holds the movable part of the cage, which is called the door, to the immovable part."

I made a hook with my index finger and pulled it against my thumb. "Like this, you see?"

"Like a tooth . . . ," he said.

"Right!"

" . . . in a skull."

"Uh, yes," I replied. "A little like that."

I took another step back from the cage. "Little pins are attached to the hook, and if they're pressed in just the right way, then the hook becomes unlatched from the bars and the door can swing open."

The Jaguar looked annoyed.

"I swear, that's how it works! It's all inside the case, so you can't see it."

"But if it's inside the case," the Jaguar said, "how do you get your fat fingers in there to press the pins?"

"Ah," I said, fumbling in my pocket. "This is the best part of all . . . a key!" I held my house key aloft so it caught a beam of light. "These little teeth on the key"—I ran my finger down its length—"are just the right size to push the pins in the lock and unhook the latch."

"Impressive." The Jaguar bowed his head and stepped away from the door. "I believe a demonstration is in order."

"Nice try. This is the key to the lock on my house, not your cage. And I wouldn't open your lock even if I did have the key."

"Oh, I see," said the Jaguar with mock surprise. "Well,

who does have my key? Perhaps I should be speaking to him."

"My father," I said, looking him in the eyes. "Why aren't you talking to him, Jaguar? Why me?"

The Jaguar licked his paw, ignoring me. "I must say, I'm not surprised by this thing. A lock and key." He paced his cage. "A jaguar eats his fill and leaves the rest for scavengers. A man would lock up the world for himself and let it rot."

"Jaguar, answer my question." I held the lamp up to his face. "Why did you do this to me?"

He slid his wet nose between the bars. The sinew in his muscled shoulders shifted and shimmered in the light.

"Because I could, young Marlin. I've unlocked you just the same as your father does with his key." His lips parted in a smile. "Man is different from the animals because he wills himself to be so. Most men's heads are buried in the ground," he purred. "But for some reason, you only had a speck of dirt in your ears. And all I did was knock it out."

"But why?" I said.

"For the same reason these foul-smelling creatures come to gawk at me in my cage. Something in you caught my eye, and I wanted to take a closer look."

He smiled, and a pleasant growl accompanied the parting of his lips. It made me feel ill.

"Perhaps we've both had enough for the night. Tomorrow we'll see what else we can learn from each other."

He turned to lick his tail, then glanced back at me.

"If what you say about the lock is true," he purred, "we should have all the time in the world."

THIRD DAY

Just when you thought your stay couldn't get any more spectacular . . . it does.

No doubt you've marveled at the surreal sight of our seven-hundred-year-old temple, ravaged by time, yet made new by the wonder set upon it by our visionary founder.

Well, count yourself among the lucky few, because the guests of this season are the first to witness Ronan Rackham's fearless second act.

A circus tent, built three hundred feet in the air, at the very pinnacle of the Great Pyramid.

The Sky Shrine promises to be the greatest circus grounds the world has ever seen. Built among the clouds, it literally looks down on all competition.

Animals of the zoo, which until now you've seen only in cages, will perform feats for your enjoyment. Traditional circus snacks like candy floss and pickled yams will be served, so save room at lunch.

Be amazed! Be enthralled! Be glad it's nothing like home!

16.

"What are you doing, Marlin?"

Olivia had cornered me at lunch and told me there was something she needed to show me. By the time I figured out she was leading me to her family's private quarters, it was too late.

I hesitated in the doorway. I wasn't allowed to be here.

"Don't worry," she said. "My parents are at lunch; they won't be back for an hour."

"Puh—PH-PFF—Dd-dd-Doe," I sputtered. I can't even tell you what I was trying to say.

She took my hand again, gently this time, and drew me into the room. I practically tripped onto the sofa where she led me.

"Just sit here and I'll get it for you." She patted my shoulder and disappeared from the main room to one of the smaller bedchambers.

I was in an estate room with the daughter of a duke, and I had pig dung on my boots. I could smell it. I had to get out of there. I stood up to leave, but before I could—

"Marlin!" She came back into the room and pressed me down onto the sofa. She sat next to me, and her weight on the cushion slightly tipped me toward her, forcing me to grab the arm of the sofa to keep myself away.

"This is what I wanted you to see," she said cheerfully. There was a leather portfolio on her lap. She unclasped the latch and took out various colored papers. They were clippings from newspapers and magazines. In one sleeve there was a tiny pulp novel.

"This is my collection," she said. "About Guiana and the zoo. In our carriage the other day, you didn't seem to know how famous you are." She pulled out a map of the country that marked several points of interest: Georgetown, the Demerara River, and a big silver star labeled THE ZOO AT THE EDGE OF THE WORLD. She leafed through a magazine story that featured sketches of the Grand Gate, the pyramid, the Great Hall, and some very inaccurate drawings of animals.

I pointed out the tusks of the elephant with my finger and shook my head.

"Yes, they've inverted them," Olivia said. "The magazine sketchers are the worst. Look at how they've drawn the tamarins." She flipped to a picture of a whole host of monkeys like Kenji that were battling a crocodile.

We both laughed at that.

"Most people like animals only if they're fighting," Olivia said. "They love the danger of it all. But I just like looking at them. Don't you, Marlin?"

I raised my eyes to her and nodded.

"It's like your father says in the book—oh, that's so strange!" Olivia shivered from head to toe. "Ronan Rackham is your father! Well, like he says in the book, 'There's no thrill so great as seeing what your eyes were never meant to!'"

She picked up the pulp novel and held it to her heart. "And now, I'm here to see it too! Goodness, I hope we stay."

"Wh-wuh-wuh?" I managed.

"This?" She touched the novel with her other hand. "It's the book about your father. Haven't you seen it?"

I shook my head.

"Oh, I can't believe he never showed you! I'm sure he's just being humble; he's very humble in the book. You simply must read it."

She thrust it into my hands. *The Amazing Adventures of Ronan Rackham* by T. S. Whitehead. The name I recognized as the man from Georgetown who wrote up our brochures.

"Ca-cc—can I buh—bh—buh?" I stammered.

"Borrow it? Of course! You can have it! I've got another copy back home."

I looked at the book in my hands. Father had always been a great mystery to me, partly because it was so hard for me to ask questions, and I think partly by his own design. He was like a great chamber door that I always wished would open but was locked to me. I felt as if Olivia had just handed me a key.

"Oh my goodness, Marlin," Olivia said. "What's happened to you?"

She pulled the book away and took hold of my right hand, flipping it over to reveal the strange, new skin.

"Uh—bu—bub—" I stuttered incoherently. Once again I had nothing to say.

She pulled my hand closer to her and my body followed. We were just inches away from each other. "So strange," she said, running her fingers over my palm. The plump skin was extra sensitive, and shivers of sensation shot through my body. "It's like a baby's." She looked up at me, and our gazes locked.

For a long moment, I was lost in her green eyes as her fingers slowly drew a circle on my palm. I felt myself leaning closer to her. She was coming toward me as well. We were definitely getting nearer, and I could smell her breath. It had a hint of chive and eggs, but it was warm and close.

"What is going on?" a harsh voice spun me around on the sofa. "You!" the duchess shouted, storming into the chambers.

Her lips were bloodred and she bared her teeth.

"Mummy, don't shout," Olivia scolded.

 "Don't you tell me what to do, young lady. You were supposed to be looking at animals!"

"I wanted to show Marlin my clippings."

The duke stepped between his wife and his daughter. "This is not proper, Olivia, no matter how innocent. Marlin, I think you should leave."

"You are in the chambers of a duchess," her mother told me coolly. "Your father will be hearing about this."

"No need to involve the captain," said the duke, giving his wife an odd look.

I was already up and twitching nervously. The duchess was in the doorway, blocking my escape.

"Sss-s-ss-sccu—zz—" I sputtered.

"Yes, excuse you," mocked the duchess, and cleared the way for me to leave.

The door slammed shut behind me in the hall, and I stood there for a minute, shivering. There was electricity shooting in my palm where Olivia had touched it, and I jammed my hand into my pocket along with the book.

17.

"Ladies and gentlemen, welcome to the Circus at the Edge of the World!"

Father was dressed in a red tailcoat with gold cufflinks and a green top hat. I'd never seen him in such an outfit in my life. But when he cracked the long, black whip in his hands, the audience of guests cheered. They were packed into the first few rows of stone bleachers in the Sky Shrine. Tim stood beside Father in the pit below. He wore black trousers and a green shirt and mouthed along to Father's lines.

My job was to "ensure the guests' safety" up in the stands. But it was just a polite way of sparing me from having to address the crowd.

I made sure to situate myself far from where the Bradshires were sitting but watched Olivia out of the corner of my eye. She was faced forward the entire time, enthralled with the circus.

"You've journeyed a long way," Father bellowed. "You've seen the splendors of the jungle. You've experienced the sights and sounds of its strange and entrancing animals. Now prepare to see them uncaged!"

Father signaled to Zargo and Manray, who were standing at the back of the pit. With one great heave, they swung open a wooden door, and Longsnout and Bottlebee, our two tapirs, came in. A tapir is a jungle animal that looks like a tall pig but has a short, movable snout similar to an elephant's. The gentle creatures looked scared, and the tail of the whip struck Bottlebee as he rushed forward.

"Please welcome the Talented Tapirs!" Father shouted. It wasn't clear what talent they had, as they were merely being chased around the pit by Zargo and Manray.

"Why are they doing this?" Kenji asked from my shoulder. "They're just running in a circle."

"I don't know, Kenj. The guests seem to like it."

"Yeah. How come you're not sitting with that girl?" Kenji asked. "She's right over there. You want Kenji to get her?"

"No." I grabbed her by the tail before she could run off. "Not right now."

The tapirs disappeared out the back door and Dreyfus, the elephant, entered trumpeting.

"What did he say?" Kenji asked, looking confused. Dreyfus's sound didn't make sense to me either. It seemed like a noise he was forced to make, so it didn't have any meaning.

It was strange learning how this all worked.

Tim snapped his fingers and the elephant went down on one knee. He placed his boot on Dreyfus's leg and took hold of his trunk. Then Dreyfus swung him up onto his head, where Tim sat between the elephant's ears. The crowd loved this, and even I couldn't help but be impressed. I didn't know Tim could work like that with an animal. Dreyfus's eyes rolled up in his head, trying to keep track of Tim's swinging boots, which were carelessly dangling in front of his face.

The elephant seemed worried, but Tim was exultant. The guests cheered him on. I even caught Olivia applauding. I wondered if she thought knowing Tim would be just as exciting as knowing me. He was a Rackham too. And he could actually talk to her.

The other acts were all the same. Animals were ushered in, made to run around or be stood on, and then ushered out again. I'd never seen a real circus, but I'd read about them, and they seemed like more grand affairs, with clowns and acrobats and bears that rode unicycles. Our circus was just a circle where animals were let out of their cages.

Later in the show, Father stepped to the center of the pit. "Clear the stage!" he bellowed, and everyone left, even Tim.

"Thank you, ladies and gentlemen," he called above the crowd. "I like to think you've enjoyed yourselves, but I know the truth." He bowed his head sadly. "Our circus is but a little thing."

The crowd whistled at this.

"No, no, it's true," Father repeated. "We can't compare to the big top at Banister and West or any of the touring shows in England. We have no special acts, and our animals are trained to do little more than run in circles." Murmurs of laughter from the crowd. Father smiled.

"I also know that you good people did not travel to the countryside for your holiday. You journeyed here, to Guiana, and that makes you a different breed. You came to find something that no longer exists in the old countries. You came to the Zoo at the Edge of the World. Here, we aim to impress.

"And impress we shall."

The door at the back of the circus pit opened and the audience fell still. In the silence could be heard the creaking of metal on metal and the shouts of men.

A black iron cage whined its way through the door on rusty axles. The wheels were chipped and uneven, and the entire cage rattled with each turn.

Inside the mobile carrier were the three apes: Trébone, Blue Boy, and Screecher. Trébone sat there silently while the others climbed the bars and pounded the ceiling.

"What is your father doing with those guys?" Kenji asked. I could only shrug. No other animals had been brought out in cages.

"The chimpanzee and the orangutan," Father began. "Marvelous creatures both. Stronger than most men and no less than half as clever, they are the knights of the jungle. They live in clans that number as high as a hundred and will fight wars over territory. They are powerful, savage creatures."

Manray was pushing the cage around the pit when Blue Boy leaped at him, reaching his thick hand between the bars. Manray dodged just in time to avoid having his vest ripped off by the chimp, and he tumbled to the ground. The audience gasped and applauded.

"Yes, these are indeed the knights of the jungle," Father said. "But this, ladies and gentlemen, is the king."

More grinding metal came from the doorway. The crowd's cheering quieted as they waited to see what would emerge. Even I leaned forward.

From the darkness came the Jaguar, bracing himself inside the bouncing cage, silent.

The guests around me rose to their feet. I could no longer see the pit for all the people in front of me.

"Of course, we all know the zoo's newest resident," Father continued. "The natives believe jaguars descend from a god. Take one look and you'll see what inspires the notion." He turned and admired the Jaguar. "It's a terrible beast. This one killed an employee of mine; that's why we captured him. Once they develop a taste for human flesh . . ." He smiled.

A collective gasp came from the crowd.

"Not to worry!" he said cautiously. "This wall is too tall for him to jump. Once we let them loose, they won't be able to leave the pit." A murmur rose throughout the crowd. "Oh yes," Father said, his eyes growing dark. "This is the finale of our show."

"Battle of the Beasts!" cried Tim, running through the back door and into the center of the pit. Father turned quickly to say something to him, but I hardly noticed. My heart was going crazy inside my chest. The skin on the palm of my right hand burned.

"A jaguar's bite is the strongest in the world." Father kept his calm, though the crowd was wild around him. "It can crack an alligator's skull. How will it fare against three vicious apes?"

"Battle to the death!" Tim shouted again. I didn't know what to do. Men were pulling sacks of silver and gold from their belts, making bets on who would win. I didn't understand; these animals were in our protection. This went against every rule my father had ever given me.

The Jaguar looked calmly into the crowd. Was he searching for me?

The apes were raging against the bars. They knew what was happening. And they knew they wouldn't stand a chance against a full-grown jaguar.

"Marlin!" Trébone hooted desperately. "Marlin!"

I had given them my word they wouldn't be hurt, but my word was worthless, just like Blue Boy had said. I couldn't control my father or anything at all. I couldn't even save the little capybara.

I steeled myself and squeezed between the two men in front of me. I would jump down into the pit. They couldn't release the animals if I was in the circle. Father would be furious, but I didn't care.

An elbow checked me across the forehead and my vision went dim. The guests were packed too closely; they'd all moved to the innermost ring of the stands, and I couldn't break through. I crouched and made to crawl between a tangle of legs, but a heavy boot crunched my hand and sent me scrambling back.

There was no way through the rabble. I wasn't strong enough to barrel through them, and I didn't have the voice to shout them down. I cast about desperately.

The big circus tent above us hung from two tall beams crossing the center of the pit. There were six support beams radiating out from the center to the back edge of the stands. The tent itself was made of wicker weave we'd bought from the tribe in exchange for a few guns.

I'd seen the tribesmen light the wicker on fire in little pits to use as smoke signals. It burned dark and smelly, but very slow. If I could set a small fire in the corner of the tent, it would smoke up the entire circus. I leaped up the stands to the back of the Sky Shrine and lifted the bottom of the wicker tent, rolling out on the ground.

The sun was hot and the sky was clear. The roar of the crowd came right through the tent and pressed me to work fast.

I hopped down the steps of the pyramid to the nearest exhibit, where there were three torches. We had them burning all around the zoo to keep out malarial mosquitoes.

The nearest torch happened to be burning next to the Sloth Cage, where Minxy was hanging upside down on his tree. He blinked at me. "Hello there, Marlin," he said as I wrenched the torch from the stand.

"Don't tell anyone," I said, and bounded back up the steps to the corner of the Sky Shrine.

The torch flame was big and long, and I guarded it with my hand as I made my ascent. When I reached the corner where the massive wicker tent was pegged into the stone, I crouched and carefully let the flame lick itself upon the fabric.

"Catch," I whispered. "Catch."

"Master Marlin! What are you doing?" Kenji bounded to my side and tried to blow out the flame. I pushed her away.

"Are you crazy?" she shrieked.

"I've got to stop that show," I said. "Do you have a better idea?"

"Oh, Master Marlin." Kenji hopped up and down. "Oh no, oh no."

The wicker browned. Then smoked. Soon, the yellow fire was dancing on the surface of the tent, growing bigger. I dropped the torch and guarded the fledgling flame with my hands, covering it so closely that it burned the skin on my right palm. But it was stronger now, and a light wind

123

was blowing it gradually upward. Soon smoke would spew into the tent.

I grabbed the now-extinguished torch and raced it back to its place by the Sloth Cage with Kenji following behind.

"Torch went out," said Minxy.

"Don't worry, there'll be enough fire to keep mosquitoes away."

I leaped back up the Pyramid stone and sprinted to the opposite corner of the Sky Shrine. Once I'd rolled under the tent flap, I could see the first plumes of smoke rising on the other side.

Father and the men were tying lines to the doors of the cages so they could pull them open from a safe distance. They were just about to clear the pit when Father froze. He could smell the smoke.

Then a cry went up from a guest. "Fire!"

The Jungle Look was on Father's face. He saw the flames now and waved the men away from the edges of the pit. "Put it out!" he shouted. "Cut it down!" But the smoke was everywhere now.

A wall of flames rose up before me. A swoosh of hot air blew my hair back. The entire east flap of the tent was writhing with fury. Black smoke streamed out along the top of the tent, and the flames roared like a demon.

I didn't know what had happened. The wicker was supposed to burn smoky and slow. I had seen it a dozen times. I was there when Father bought it. Then I remembered a conversation he'd had with Drake Mandrian, a leader of the tribesmen. Father wanted the tent waterproofed so it wouldn't leak in the rainy season and ruin his shows.

He gave the tribe whale fat to coat it with. The same stuff we used in our oil lamps.

A towering swath of burning tent tore away from its support and collapsed on a cluster of guests. They rolled on the ground and swatted at themselves to put out the burning wicker strands. Ash came down like snow, and the crowd pressed toward the main exit near where I was at the back of the tent.

The stream of guests rushed by me, and suddenly Olivia was there, grabbing my arm. "Come with us, Marlin!"

I pulled away from her and shouted, "G—gg—go!"

A man covered in ash nearly knocked me over, and I moved away from the crush of guests. The air was hot and it hurt to breathe. I crouched low to avoid the smoke and hopped down the steps of the bleachers toward the edge of the pit. The drop was fifteen feet, but I didn't hesitate. I landed feetfirst and my ankles nearly went numb from the pain.

Father and his men were desperately pushing the apes' and the Jaguar's cages toward the great wooden door to the back of the Sky Shrine.

Soon I was at Father's side, heaving the Jaguar's cage over the lumpy dirt. I sensed the Jaguar looking at me, but I was ashamed and could not make eye contact.

"You lied, boy!" Blue Boy screamed from his bouncing carrier. His fangs were bared and he smashed against the bars so violently, I feared he'd break out and throttle me. Screecher was next to him, shaking and foaming at the mouth. Trébone just stared at me.

"I'll kill you for this!" Blue Boy called.

Father didn't acknowledge me when I joined him, but a piece of smoldering wicker fell behind my ear and he brushed it away.

The men pushing the ape carrier got through the wooden door first. Father and I struggled with the weight of the cage and the uneven ground. My breath was ragged and my arms felt full of blood. Another section of burning tent tore free and landed behind us with a roar.

The Jaguar reclined calmly in his cage, and we finally made it through the doors and into safety and the sunlight.

"So this is a circus," he purred. "I have to admit, it was very entertaining."

THIRD NIGHT

We're sure that performance left you breathless. With wild beasts just a stone's throw away, you'd have to be dead to not be thrilled. But here at the Zoo at the Edge of the World, we make it our business to marry death and danger with safety and splendor.

After a day of thrills, expect a night of delights: a candlelight soiree by our Reflecting Pool, and an ice-cream social in the Great Hall. But you needn't choose just one—they're both open until midnight!

And if you're wondering how our animal trainers worked their magic with the animals in the circus ring, there will be a special presentation after dinner starring your master of ceremonies, Ronan Rackham, and his top staff. Listen closely: he may have some tips on how to train your little ones back home.

18.

"You find out who's responsible, you bring them to me!" Father commanded no one in particular. "Someone set fire to that tent."

The heads of all the work groups were in his office. Tim and I stood shoulder to shoulder with the thirteen crew captains. Everyone was solemn. I tried to keep from shaking.

Father was standing hunched over his desk, hair in his face, mustache beaded with sweat. I glanced at Tim, who stared straight ahead, hard faced. Zargo was to my left, strong and calm, but the ragged breaths around me betrayed the other men's fear. I felt it overwhelming me. My right hand burned with fire, and I had to clench it in a tight fist to keep from screaming.

"Sabotage, yeah?" His voice was a torn whisper. "We had a traitor here last week, Nathtam Leent." Father referred to the man who had led the strike and was killed by the Jaguar.

"Luck doesn't favor traitors."

A snort sounded to the left of me. It was Leedo Flute.

"Something funny?" Father asked, deadly serious.

Leedo quickly swallowed whatever had been on the tip of his tongue and said, "No, sir."

"Are you laughing at me?" Father raised up to his full height. The air seemed to leave the room. "Do you wish I weren't here, Leedo, bothering you with this . . . petty concern?" Father took one step toward him. That was all it took.

"No, sir—no, not at all." Leedo bowed his head. "I've respect for you, sir, utmost respect. I'm so very sorry."

"He's lying," Tim said, stepping forward.

"What?" Leedo asked, sweating. "No."

"I heard him the other day, taunting Marlin," Tim continued. "He told him he hoped that you didn't return from your hunt. That the jaguar would kill you."

"I did not!" Leedo shouted, but Father was already on him. He grabbed Leedo by the shirt and rammed him against the wall.

"Want me dead, huh?" He rocked him against the wood beams. "Want to burn down my zoo?"

Leedo hadn't done anything. I deserved the punishment. Part of me wanted to be in my father's grip, for him to shake and strike me for what I'd done and all the people I'd endangered. But another part wanted to strike him back, to stand over him and shout that he was a bully and a blowhard and that he'd gone back on his word. These animals were ours to protect, he always said so, not to turn on each other for entertainment.

I felt the words boiling up in my throat. My palm ached, and the pain propelled me forward. But I was caught at the back of my collar by a big, strong hand. Zargo pulled me back and wrapped another arm around my chest. "Leave it," he whispered to me.

"What do you have to say for yourself?" Father bellowed.

"It was the jaguar!" Leedo's lips pulled back as he pronounced each word, and flecks of spit sprayed my father's face. "It is a curse he laid on us for bringing him here. What we did was wrong, and this is punishment."

Father pulled back slightly, unnerved by Leedo's words. Zargo Hunt stepped in front of me and echoed him. "It's true. The jaguar laid a curse."

Father released Leedo and stared blankly. "You're saying a jaguar set the fire?" His eye rolled around the room. "An animal?"

"Animal has power," said one of the men.

"A curse," said another.

One by one all the men were casting blame. "The jaguar!" they shouted. "We must kill it!"

Father turned away from the crush of men. "I won't have you giving me orders."

"Mr. Rackham," Zargo spoke up. "How can you deny—"

"I deny what I wish!" Father bellowed. "I will not harbor superstition. And I will not be governed by fear. I'll throw you all in a cage." He pounded his fist on his desk. "Then you will tell me what happened to my circus!"

The room went quiet. The men feared the jaguar, but Father was the more present threat.

"That cat will not turn my zoo into a jungle. We are civilized here!" He stamped his foot. "Tim, Marlin, come here."

We broke ranks with the workers and went to our father's side. He put one massive hand on each of our shoulders.

"My boys will be guarding the jaguar's den from now on. None of you goes near it until I find out who burned my circus."

"I volunteer for first watch, Father!" Tim barked in a soldier's voice. Father considered him.

"Marlin will watch the den tonight," he said, squeezing my shoulder.

"But I'm the oldest," Tim protested. "That's not right!"

"Who holds the Paw?" Father said. "We run this zoo on merit. You want fairness? Become a lawyer."

Father turned to me. "You can do it, Son," he whispered. Behind him, Tim burned with rage.

But I still nodded.

"I know you can." Father winked and dismissed the men. They crept out of the small office, sullen and shaken, muttering to themselves. Tim glared at me. I half suspected he knew what I'd done. But that was impossible. He was only jealous.

No one knew the truth. Father smiled at me. My right palm was seared with burning fire.

I smiled back.

19.

The Jaguar lay silent across the darkened room. Father had outfitted me with a rifle and bayonet to ward off intruders. It wasn't the first time I'd held a gun, but I wasn't much of a shot. I didn't like blowing apart the coffee cans we used for practice, and I'd never hunted something living. How could I protect the Jaguar if someone came for him? I adjusted my grip on the barrel.

Father and I entered the Ruby Palace, and the light of the oil lamp twinkled in the hundred bits of glass. But their glimmer was diminished somehow, not as bright as it had been the night before. There was rain in the air, heavy and thick, and the lamp struggled to light the damp darkness.

Father told me where to stand and positioned the rifle in my hands. He kicked my feet together, told me to stand up straight.

"If anyone comes, shout, 'Halt!'" Father said. "Fire a warning shot at his feet. If that doesn't stop him, aim for the chest." He addressed me like a soldier. "Understood?"

I nodded my head.

"The bayonet," he added taking the rifle from my hand, "is used in close quarters, if a shot to the chest isn't enough to stop him. Slash to push him back and then jab."

I blinked my eyes rapidly, trying to hide my fear. But Father saw it. He set down the gun and knelt.

"I know this isn't the way you'd prefer things to be." The skin around his eyes crinkled, and a pained smile formed under his mustache. "Tim's the warrior in the family. He's got that part of me. And I know it isn't easy for you, living with him. He's hard on you, just like everyone else."

My face felt flush and a lump rose up in my throat. I turned away from Father, but he put a finger to my chin and drew me back to him. "Do you ever wonder why I don't stop him when he's cruel to you?"

My head grew hot and I was very afraid I would start to cry, because I did wonder that. I had wondered it my entire life. My father was the strongest man in the world, but he never stopped anyone from being cruel to me.

"It's because Tim's got the warrior in me, but you've got something else. And though no one has ever expected much from you, I've always known something was there." Tears filled his eyes then, and ran along the crinkles. "When you walked out of that cage with those apes, everyone saw it. You've got the best part of me, son."

Tears were in my eyes too, though I couldn't say if they

were from pride or fear.

"I know you'll do great things," Father said, handing me the gun.

I blinked the tears away and nodded my head.

When Father left, the Jaguar stopped pretending to be asleep. We looked at each other but said nothing.

We must have spent several hours in silence, because eventually the antbirds began to sing. They only do that just before dawn.

"I should say I'm sorry," I said.

The Jaguar didn't respond. He reclined lazily, his paw beneath his chest, looking up at the flickering oil lamp. A cloud of gnats hovered around the flame.

"I mean to say, I'm sorry for what happened today. My father and the circus. I'm the one who lit the fire."

The Jaguar blinked his eyes. "I know," he said.

"Father's furious. He thinks it was one of the men."

"I see."

"But the men say it was you. They say holding you here is a curse, and we should kill you. That's why Father has me standing guard."

"I see that, too."

The Jaguar's uninterest enraged me.

"If you see so bloody much, how come you're in this cage? How come you killed Nathtam and caused all this trouble?" I realized I was pointing the rifle toward him. The blade of the bayonet poked through the bars of his cage. The Jaguar considered its tip.

"I've just puzzled something out," he said.

"What?" I sighed and withdrew the bayonet.

The Jaguar perked up, his yellow eyes squinting. "Since you came here, I've been confused by that lamp. I thought it was captured moonlight. And I've wondered about those insects that circle the flame."

He lifted his eyebrow at the lamp and the cloud of gnats that surrounded the light. "They fly around and around, crashing into each other, and then they get too close and poof, they're gone."

I wasn't really in the mood for questions. I said, "Bugs just do that. I don't know why."

"There's a reason for every action," the Jaguar responded. "Today, I watched men flee from fire in terror, and I thought, 'Why does the gnat fly toward it?'"

"Because they're stupid," I said. "I don't know. I can't talk to bugs."

"Yes, they're too simple to speak with us. But simplicity does not lack reason."

"Then why?" I said. "Do you know?"

"The reason the gnats circle the flame," the Jaguar said as another bug burst into vapor, "is because they make the same mistake I did. They think it's the moon."

"So bugs want to fly into the moon?"

"No," he said. "At night, insects navigate by the position

of the moon. If they can keep it to one side of them, they know they're heading straight."

"Huh," I said. "That's how sailing ships do it too, you know. Except they use the stars."

"For all the years since the world was made, that is how the insects kept their flight. And for eons, it worked, because there were no bright lights besides the moon. Then man came and worked out a way to light the night. The gnats that see your flame mistake it for the moon, and, as they've done since the dawn of time, they try to keep it to one side."

I looked up at the cloud of tiny bugs, all circling the flame like planets around the sun.

"But the fire is so much closer than the moon," I said. "So when they fly by it, they've got to turn to keep it in the same place."

"And circle round and round chasing it," the Jaguar purred. "And in their frenzy, they bump into their friends and grow confused. So attracted are they to the light that they fly closer and closer, maddened by its ancient pull, and are swallowed in the heat."

"That's a shame," I said.

Another gnat burst into smoke. The crackling noise made me wince.

"The simple instincts of that gnat drove him true in the night. But now, with the machines of man, his basic nature does him in. We are all governed by instinct. But like the gnat's, man's instincts have been warped by his machines, as you call them. Look at the lock. All of us need to eat and store our food. But once you give a creature a lock, he thinks, 'I can capture all the prey in the forest and lock it up for my pleasure.' Instead of taking what he can eat and enjoy, he strives to take it all and locks up the entire world."

"Sounds like a king," I said. "They want to own everyone and everything."

"Yes," the Jaguar purred. "And what happens when two kings meet?"

"There's war," I said.

The Jaguar nodded his head. "We kill to eat in the jungle. But there are no locks and cages. There is no war."

I thought of my father. He was the king of this place, and that made me a prince. One day I'd get the keys to all the locks.

I turned to the Jaguar. "You told me people choose to be apart from the animals. Was there a time before when we were the same?"

"I was not around before, so I don't know." The Jaguar flashed his eyes. "Most men's tongues go unused, but you're unique. I gave you this gift, Marlin, because you could receive it."

I didn't feel well. My hands were shaking. Another gnat burst into flames, and the crack of its body breaking apart set off a panic in me. "I don't want to be a king," I said. "And I don't want to hurt anyone. But ever since you've given me this power, I feel like I'm doing it all the time. I fail my father; I fail the animals. Tell me what I should do."

He slid one enormous paw between the bars of his cage and curled the other around the lock. He licked his nose, and for a moment I felt hunted.

"You can let me out."

His ears were peaked. His nostrils flared slightly, taking in my scent, and his haunches flexed. He was a curtain of black that could draw over me in an instant, snuffing me out.

The gun rattled in my hand.

"I can't do that," I said.

"Of course you can." He raised his voice slightly.

"I don't have the key."

"You can get it," he snarled. "Free me and all the others. End this nightmare of confinement."

"No, I won't," I said, taking a step back. "This place is my home. These animals are my friends."

"Friends you keep under lock and key?" the Jaguar said.

"This place is my father's," I said, feeling indignant. "It's not mine. I can't do that. It would kill him."

"Then what's the alternative?" the Jaguar retorted. "Killing me?"

"You're safe here!" I said. "We'll protect you. That's *why* you're here. To show everyone there's nothing to be afraid of!"

I parroted my father's words with tears in my eyes. I had always believed them.

"Marlin!" Tim's voice called from beyond the door of the Ruby Palace. He was early.

"That's my brother," I said, taking the lamp from the hook. "We'll protect you. I swear it."

The Jaguar considered me silently. I wiped my eyes and opened the door.

FOURTH DAY

Break out of the resort today, and immerse yourself in the freedom and beauty of Guiana. Probe the dark depths of the jungle and see what it means to be truly wild.

But in luxury, of course! Catch a ride on the *Saint of the Animals*, the gloriously appointed riverboat that brought you here. After breakfast, meet at the docks and take a journey even farther up the river. Spot crocodiles and swinging tree monkeys in their natural habitat. Sing along with the macaws and throw fish to the manatees.

For the truly adventurous, hop into one of our rowboats and take an excursion up the river with an experienced guide. This is not for the faint of heart!

If that all seems a bit much, relax back at the zoo instead. The buffet will be open all day, each meal accompanied by the civilizing strains of our house band. Take in the gardens and the Butterfly House, and visit all the animals you haven't yet had a chance to see. This is your last full day in the Zoo at the Edge of the World. Make it the best one.

20.

Tim pulled me outside and shut the door to the Ruby Palace behind me.

"You look well rested," he said blankly. "Have a nap in there, did you?"

I scowled at him and handed over the gun. "I ST-sss—ST-staaa—"

"Save it," he said with a wave of his hand. "Get to bed."

The door to the Ruby Palace had locked automatically when Tim closed it. I sighed and began to fumble with the key.

"I've got the key." Tim pushed my hand away.

I stood there waiting for him to unlock the door and go inside. He was a full hour early, and Father had told us I wasn't supposed to leave until Tim had gone in. I gestured for him to go through the door.

"Are you deaf as well?" Tim glared at me. "I said get to bed!"

"AH-ah-AH-ar-ar-aren't . . ."

"Aren't I what?" Tim said. "I don't have to explain myself to you now, do I? God, this place is a joke." Tim pressed his finger into my ribcage. "Once this place is mine, first thing I'll do is fire you, you little snot!"

I put my hand around his finger and moved it away from my chest. I gestured again for him to go inside. His eyes widened. "Got a problem listening to what I say?" He pushed me, and I almost fell backward. "You don't want to get in my way today."

I stepped up to him. He was a full foot taller than me, and he leaned down, breathing onto my forehead. I sensed he was about to hit me.

But I didn't care.

"Bah—Bah—Bah—Bah!" I stammered furiously. "Kk-ku-ku-k-KK-KK-KK!" My tongue cracked against the top of my throat. "Ssss-Swuh—Ssss-Swhuh!" My mouth twisted into a terrible shape, and I spewed half words at him.

You've been a terrible brother. You've never been a friend to me. I try to be nice to you, and you spit in my face. Even Father knows what a rage-fueled brat you are!

It didn't matter to me that I couldn't form the words. It didn't matter that I was an incomprehensible mute. I was loud, I was angry, and I made my meaning clear.

I am not a mute.

Tim blinked and pulled back slightly. I'd surprised him, and he didn't know what to do. There was spittle on his face, and he wiped it off with the sleeve of his shirt. He opened his mouth. Then he closed it again. For once, he had nothing to say.

I turned from him and trotted down the steps of the Golden Path. Too much had happened in the last few days for me to care about petty arguments with Tim. I was tired. I wanted to go to bed and dream of something else.

The bedsheets were sticky and hot. There was no sleeping during the day in the jungle, and that's why everyone did all they could to avoid night shifts. I ripped the cotton sheets off my straw mattress to try to get cool, but the prickly mattress scratched my skin raw. The sun was on fire and there was no rest for me that morning.

I trudged my way to the Great Hall for breakfast. The guests were in their fancy day clothes, while my hair was matted with bits of straw, and my work shirt stuck to my skin. But I didn't care what I looked like to them.

From the corner of my eye, I saw Father breakfasting awkwardly at a table with the duke and duchess, and I regretted ever leaving bed. I tried to make my way back to the exit, but he spotted me.

"Marlin," Father called from the table. "Marlin, come join us." He had a chair pulled out for me next to him.

"Good morning, soldier," he said loud enough for them both to hear. "Looks like you've had a trying night."

The duke and duchess didn't take the bait. They had no

145

interest in what I'd done to look so terrible.

"Marlin stood guard all night," Father said. "Gave you an appetite, eh, boy?" He clapped his hand on my back and summoned the waiter to bring me some potatoes and bacon.

"You work him entirely too hard," the duke said, trying to be polite.

"Yes." The duchess arched her eyebrow. "He's a busy boy."

"He's going to own this zoo one day. Won't you, Marlin?" Father smiled broadly at me. He put a hand on my shoulder as though he expected me to respond. He'd never tried to engage me in conversation in front of guests before.

"That would be something to see," the duchess said, and clucked her tongue.

Father looked at her blankly. "How do you mean, Your Grace?"

The duke elbowed her, but she wasn't going to stop.

"He'll need to learn a few things about courtesy first." The duchess chuckled to herself. "For example, how to say hello!"

The duke turned red. I saw a look of contempt on Father's face.

"My boy is more than competent," Father said quietly. "This is a family business and will be run by my family always."

"Hear, hear!" The duke raised his glass, trying to cut the tension. "To your family business! May it be ever fruitful."

"Yes," the duchess said. "We are so lucky that we only have a girl and don't need to worry about her career. She'll marry the right man someday." She looked at me directly. "Someone highborn, of course."

Just then the server delivered our plates. Bacon and potatoes for all.

"But what about your family business right here?" Father leaned over the table.

"Pardon me?" asked the duke.

"Your new venture in Guiana," he said, taking a bite of bacon. "Buying up land for a sugar forest?"

The duke stiffened, as did the duchess. They turned almost imperceptibly toward each other as though they could consult through telepathy. Father looked up from his plate and gave a broad smile.

"I don't know where you'd hear something like that," the duke said unconvincingly. "I'm not even sure what that means. A 'sugar forest' . . . are you familiar with that term, my dear?" The duchess's skin tone began to match her rouge.

"I have a few friends in town. In the land offices." Father buttered his toast, calm as could be. "Bids like that for jungle acreage don't go unnoticed, Your Grace. I know you're an intelligent man; please don't pretend otherwise."

The duke wiped the corner of his mouth with a cloth napkin and pushed away his plate. The duchess was watching him carefully, but now he ignored her.

"You've done well with this resort, old boy. But it's time

for these lands to be developed. If someone can do it profitably and safely . . ."

"It is being used profitably and safely," retorted Father.

The duke laughed. "I have no doubts of your profits, Captain. But judging from yesterday's events, I'd hardly call this resort safe."

"That fire was a fluke," said Father, growing heated. "I spent half my life exploring this jungle, the other half building this zoo. And I'll be cursed if I'm going to watch you burn it to raise sugarcane."

Father slammed his palm on the table and shook the silverware. For a moment, everyone was quiet, even the duchess.

"So you're the other bidder," the duke said stiffly. "Buying up the parcels between my parcels so I can't get a connected tract. We shall see what Governor Hincks has to say about you stifling progress in this colony."

"Yes, and we shall see what he has to say about over-reaching nobles bribing my employees to strike and shut me down."

"What did you say?" the duchess gasped. "What did you just say to him?"

Olivia appeared at the table beside her father and gave everyone a start. "Daddy, what's going on?"

The duke threw a glance to his wife. "Nothing, darling, nothing. I'm sorry. Please sit with us."

He pulled out a chair, and Olivia sat down cautiously.

"How are you, Marlin? Captain Rackham?" she greeted me and Father.

"Very well, miss," Father said.

I nodded and gave a slight smile.

"Did you just wake up, my dear?" the duke asked.

"No . . . ," Olivia answered cautiously. "In fact, Captain Rackham, I'm glad to see you. I wanted to ask what time the jaguar exhibit opens."

"It opened at eight a.m.," Father answered. "Just as the others did."

"Well, that's what I thought," Olivia said, looking puzzled.

"What do you mean, my angel?" the duchess asked, trying to sound cheery.

"It's eight thirty now," said Olivia, looking at her pocket watch, "and I was just at the Ruby Palace. But the door was locked."

Father and I turned to each other slowly, both hesitant to make eye contact and confirm what we already knew.

21.

Father fired his pistol when Tim didn't answer the door to the Ruby Palace. The bullet blew the bolt half out of the jamb. He reached into the splintered mass of wood and wrenched it the rest of the way, then kicked the heavy frame. Slivers of split wood and bent metal jammed the door, but another kick swung it open.

Tim lay on the floor of the den. Father rushed into the enclosure, and I followed with Zargo Hunt. Manray Light-foot was keeping the Bradshires outside—they had insisted on coming with us—and I could hear him saying something in Arawak.

Was Tim crying? I couldn't be sure. He buried his face in his shoulder and clutched an open wound on his forearm. Cloth and flesh mixed in a bloody pulp. I had to look away.

The Jaguar paced his cage, breathing heavily. As he walked, red prints came off his forepaws.

The rifle was lying halfway inside the Jaguar's cage, the barrel pointed toward him. The bayonet had snapped off and lay bloodstained at the Jaguar's feet.

Father was at Tim's side. "What happened?" he shouted. Tim didn't respond but only buried his face farther in his shoulder.

"Help me!" Father commanded, and Zargo went to his side. I hovered over the three of them, unsure of what to do.

"Let me see the wound," Zargo said.

"Keep off me," Tim snarled.

"We need to see it," Father said. Tim unclenched his hand from the wound, and Father probed it with his finger. Tim cried out in pain, but Father didn't stop. I suppose he realized what had happened before I did.

"You'll live," he said taking off his over shirt and wrapping it round Tim's arm for a tourniquet, "but with the doctor gone, you'll need to go to Georgetown." Tim groaned as Father yanked the knot tight. "Maybe you'll meet a girl there. Tell her you almost killed a jaguar."

"...Marlin's fault," Tim moaned. "...left the cage open... I had to fight him...."

Father glanced at me, and I panicked. The Jaguar asked me to let him out, of course, but I never did. Could I have done it without remembering?

"How could he do that when I've got the only key?" Father said gruffly, and pulled a brass key off his belt. "How is the jaguar back in the cage? Why's the gun in there with him?"

"The . . . the workers . . . ," Tim said weakly.

Father pulled me to him and put his hand in my shirt pocket. He pulled out the Paw and turned Tim's face toward him with his boot.

"This is what you're after?" he yelled, his eyes burning.

I looked again at the rifle with the twisted bayonet, and it came clear to me. That's why Tim had changed the guard early and wanted me to leave. He'd planned to kill the Jaguar and say I'd left the cage open, forcing him to defend himself—or else that I'd abandoned my post and left the Jaguar to our superstitious employees. Either way, I would be the worthless little brother again. But the plan hadn't worked.

Father and Zargo lifted Tim by his armpits.

"It hurts!" Tim screamed. But they already had him up.

"If you can try to kill my jaguar, then you can walk," Father said to him.

With Tim in Zargo's arms, Father went to the Jaguar's cage, picked up the damaged rifle, and slammed the butt against the metal door.

The Jaguar leaped back, hissing.

"You're no curse," Father said. "You're just a bloodthirsty animal."

They stared at each other across the bars. Father pointed the dented rifle barrel at the Jaguar. I didn't know if it could still fire.

"T-ttt-TT-Tim!" I managed, and broke the standoff.

"We'll take him to the boat," Father said.

We took off toward the dock, Tim yelping all the way.

Father laid Tim in a guest cabin on *Saint of the Animals* and told the captain, an Englishman called Reese Mundy, to sail to Georgetown and deposit Tim at Victoria Hospital in the High Quarter. Charro, our healer, would make the journey with him. Father ordered Mundy to depart as soon as we were off the ship.

"There might be a problem with that," the sailor replied.

The gangplank, our bridge between the ship and solid ground, was packed with guests. Sailors were struggling to stop them from boarding.

The Duke of Bradshire stood at the front of the mob, arguing with a sailor. "I could have you hanged for this!" the duke was saying. Then he spotted my father. "Captain Rackham! We demand to be heard!"

Father looked nonplussed. "Your Grace, what is this?"

"Your zoo is dangerous, that's what!" the duke bellowed. The assembled guests called out their agreement. It was a throng of about twenty, a fifth of the guests in this week's group. Some had luggage in their arms. "We will not let this ship leave."

"It's my boy." Father took in the crowd. "He's hurt. He needs a hospital."

"That may be true." The duke turned from Father to the crowd. "But it is my sacred duty to protect my countrymen, and this resort puts English lives in danger."

The crowd sounded a note of agreement and panic. They were being turned into a mob by the duke. When Father had first said the duke had bribed our employees to strike, I hadn't believed it. But now it seemed clear to me that Olivia's father was trying to destroy our resort, though I still didn't understand why.

"Yesterday's fire was nearly deadly, and now your animals are making attacks," the duke continued. "I demand that you refund these citizens' fees and allow them to return to Georgetown this afternoon."

"Refund!" shouted a man in a souvenir safari hat.

"Take us home!" yelled a woman with a parasol.

We had to get Tim to Georgetown or his wounds could become infected.

"Your Grace and guests, please." Father tried to calm the crowd. "The zoo is safe; this week's accidents were flukes. The ship must leave now. It will be back to pick you up tomorrow evening. There is plenty more to see, and—"

"A refund!"

"Let us go!"

The duke stood at the front of the mob, entirely satisfied. The duchess and Olivia finally squeezed through to stand next to him. Olivia's brow was knitted with worry. She mouthed, "I'm sorry," to me from across the distance. I tried to summon a reassuring look for her but couldn't. I turned away bitterly.

"All right," Father relented. "You may have your refunds, and you may leave. But hear me."

The duke smugly motioned for the crowd to listen.

"This has been a trying week," Father said. "I understand your frustrations. Two new attractions have not gone as planned. I've never seen anything like it in all the years I . . ."

Father trailed off. His eyes searched for a solution that wasn't there. Refunding the guests would cost a fortune, and loading them all onto the ship would take hours. We didn't have that long.

"But—this is an extraordinary land." Father slowly raised his finger in the air. "And you have accepted an extraordinary challenge in coming here. Every adversity you have faced you conquered bravely and with dignity. Now let me give you one last challenge."

Zargo and I exchanged glances behind Father's back.

"My boy is injured, and I am sending him back to the city on this boat. Any guest who can be ready to go within the hour may join him and will be in Georgetown by midnight. Because you would be leaving one day early, I will grant each guest who elects to leave a full refund."

A sound of agreement issued from the crowd, but Father gestured to quiet them.

"But anyone who elects to stay, completing their full week at the resort, will be returned to Georgetown tomorrow night, just a few hours past their scheduled arrival, to allow the boat time to return to the zoo. And anyone who stays will be invited to a special event."

With this Father smiled for the first time, and the duke's smile began to fade.

"Tomorrow morning, before breakfast, the jaguar will be executed in the Sky Shrine. All remaining guests are invited to watch this dangerous animal meet his end. That is my offer."

The *Saint of the Animals* departed ten minutes later. Tim and the crew were the only ones on board.

FOURTH NIGHT

This will be a night to remember. All the wonderful sights you've seen and the friends you've made will come together in a last hurrah!

It's the Closing Gala, and it will end your adventure at the Zoo at the Edge of the World just as grandly as it began. The band will play, the wine will flow, and we'll dance the hours away across the ballroom floor.

Every table will be set with mementos of your time here that you may take home and display proudly, making you the envy of all your friends and relatives. But don't start reliving the good memories yet. There's still time to make new ones.

All exhibits close early so the staff can prepare the gala. But don't worry, your favorite animals will still be there tomorrow, right in the places you've left them.

22

"What this is for you is a lesson in management."

Father sat across from me at the small wooden table, chewing his beef. We were eating dinner at home tonight so Father could skip the meal at the Closing Gala. He said he'd have a lot of talking to do.

"You're seeing all that goes into an operation like this. It's big, it's complicated, and you have to play the cards that are dealt to you." Little flecks of beef had caught in Father's mustache, and he licked them out as he spoke. I hadn't touched my meal. Meat wasn't for me anymore, I decided, but I knew this wasn't the right time to mention it, so I slipped bits to Kenji under the table.

"Look at what's happened with the jaguar. There's a man-eater on the loose in the jungle," he said in mock terror. "Terrible, isn't it? No! We catch him and bring him back here, and now we've got the most amazing creature in all the wild. Everybody's mad for him. But I'm not going to just leave him in a cage for folks to gawk at. I put him in the circus show, front and center. And we give him something spectacular."

Father squinted his eyes and looked off into the distance. I suspected it wasn't just coffee in his cup.

"Of course, that didn't work out the way I'd planned. Sabotage threw us for a loop." He scowled bitterly at some imagined person over my shoulder, and I tensed up.

"I thought the jaguar was perfect for this place," Father said ruefully. "He would show the people I could make the jungle safe for them. Show them that the wild parts are what's beautiful about it, so they'd care, and not want to burn it all down to make a piece of silver."

He looked at me, but I wouldn't meet his eye. He spoke in a softer tone. "I don't want to do it, Marlin. But I have to. The workers want the jaguar dead; the guests do too. You saw them at the boat—I had to give them blood. Our job is to give the people what they want. If we don't do that, we go out of business."

I thought our job was protecting the jungle.

Father took another swig from his mug, and I passed Kenji a strip of beef.

"Don't feed that monkey at the table!" Father bellowed. He slammed his mug down.

I'd spent that afternoon in my room, alone, reading

the book Olivia had given me, *The Amazing Adventures of Ronan Rackham*. It was a quick read, and the stories were familiar to me. Father's heroic passage to South America. Father's heroic exploration of the jungle, and the building of the Zoo at the Edge of the World. Nothing about the death of my mother, or my stutter, or Tim's sadism. Just Father's best moments, the stories he tells over and over.

One thing in the book stuck out to me. Again and again the author described Father as "Ronan Rackham, Conqueror and Protector of the Jungle." Almost as if that were a title he'd been given by a king.

Father breathed heavily. "This is what we have to do."

"S-s-S-sa-SA-sooorr—y," I stuttered, without emotion.

"That's all right, my boy, that's all right." Father loudly pushed back his chair. He crept around to my side of the table, leaned over my plate, and wrapped his arms around me. His elbow was in the beef. "You're who I've got now," he said, his voice raspy with drink. "Just me and my little boy."

Ronan Rackham, Conqueror and Protector of the Jungle.

He hugged me so tight, I had to hold my breath.

23.

The gala was a strange nightmare of music and colored lights. Father entertained the guests all night, flattering the ladies and joking with the men. To everyone who visited our table he said, "You'll be at the Sky Shrine first thing tomorrow morning? It's going to be quite a show!" The guests would laugh and squeal and grow faint with excitement.

I sat there and listened to it all. Some guests wanted to know what method Father would use to dispatch the Jaguar. A gun? A spear? Some said it served the Jaguar right, attacking humans. Some were so thrilled at the chance to see a real execution that they were speechless and simply thanked my father for a wonderful week.

Out of the dozen or so dining tables set up in the Great Hall, there were only two fashionable places to be: visiting our table by the big window, or the duke's family table on the other side of the dance floor. Every guest paid a lengthy visit to each and listened to either my father or the duke hold forth. The two men tried their best to ignore each other.

While Father was entertaining a pair of blond sisters with stories of days in the jungle, I decided to leave. I quietly turned out of my chair and walked across the dance floor to the big double doors.

Olivia caught my sleeve in the garden by the exit.

"Marlin," she said, looking less than happy in her party dress. "I've got to say I'm so sorry about everything. Whatever's going on between our fathers, I need you to know it has nothing to do with us."

I turned around and looked at her skeptically. She was the one who'd been raving about her daddy's sugar forest. "Please, Marlin," she said. "I know you're upset about your brother. It's terrible what happened to him. That jaguar is just evil." She said it with such innocence. The Jaguar was the fairytale monster. Tomorrow he'd get what he deserved.

My eye twitched, and the new skin on the palm of my right hand felt raw. "N—nnn-NO!" I said. "No!"

Olivia pulled back, scared. Tears streamed down my face. She reached out to hold my hand, but I turned from her. I walked toward the Golden Path and didn't look back. She called after me, but I ignored her.

The house was dark when I got there. No one was home, not even Kenji. I lit a lamp and wandered the halls of my house like a ghost.

Eventually, I found the thing I was looking for.

24.

"If you're my guard for the evening, where's your rifle?" the Jaguar asked.

"There's no guard tonight," I said, closing the broken door as best I could. I turned the spark stone in the lamp and hung it in the center of the room. Light danced in the colored glasses, and the Jaguar purred.

"For some reason I thought I'd never see that again," he said. "I'm glad you're here."

"Jaguar, this is very serious."

"Where's your father?"

"At a party."

"Ah, yes. I can hear music, just like my first night." He sighed. "And your brother?"

"On a boat. Back to Georgetown."

"Music is the one human thing I am fond of."

"Father's going to kill you, Jaguar." I said. "In the morning."

He pricked up his ears and was silent. His massive frame slumped slightly.

"Just when I was beginning to enjoy things here."

"I hate this!" I shouted. I kicked the door of his cage and banged my fists against the bars. They didn't budge.

"Careful, little one," the Jaguar said. "I've tried that already, and it hurts."

"Why'd you have to hurt Tim?"

"He was going to kill me. I should have let him?"

"No."

"Then what?"

"You never should have come," I said. "Never should have spoken to me. Never given me this."

"I didn't come by choice." The Jaguar leaned his head against the bars of the cage, and his thick, black fur pressed through. It was soft, and I could feel it warm on my hand. "Looks like I'll die here anyway," he continued. "You want your gift to die with me? Go back to being as you were?"

"I don't know."

"You could be daddy's good boy with the broken mouth. You could be having a grand time at the gala."

"Gnats to a flame," I said bitterly.

The Jaguar laughed. "That's good. I'm glad you can speak, if only because I like talking to you."

"Is that true?"

"Well, I am a captive audience." The Jaguar chuckled. "So you wouldn't know either way."

My head was spinning, and I sat down on the stones.

The world felt very wrong in that moment. I was talking to a jaguar while Father and his guests danced in the middle of the jungle.

"I don't know what to think anymore," I said. "I don't know what I want."

The Jaguar's lips curled into a smile and his eyes went wide. "You want to let me out," he said.

I sat quietly for a moment on the stones. "You're a man-eater," I said halfheartedly.

"I am no such thing."

"Even so, there's nothing I can do."

A light wind whistled through the shot-out door of the Ruby Palace. The lamp twirled on the hook and the colored lights spun.

"I can smell a liar," the Jaguar hissed. "If you leave me here to die, the least you can do is tell the truth."

I put my right hand to my back pocket. The hard metal bulge pressed against the sensitive skin on my palm and gave me shivers. It was the key to the Jaguar's cage, taken from Father's room that night.

It had always been with him, in his pocket or on his bedpost. But he'd been talking to me as he dressed for the Gala, and when he'd changed his work clothes for a dress suit, I'd seen that he'd left the key on his belt. The rum had made him careless.

Stealing it was easy. I told myself it was nothing to take a key. It wasn't as though I intended to use it. But now, it was between my thumb and forefinger. The shining brass reflected the multicolored light. The Jaguar stepped into the shadowy corner of his cage. The room's air seemed to tighten around me like a boa constrictor.

I slid the key into the lock. The tumblers must have clicked into place, but I didn't hear them. Two different worlds were open before me.

Turn the key to the right, and the door stays locked. I am my father's son.

Turn the key to the left, and the door opens. The Jaguar. The unknown.

The key was in the center, cutting my future in two.

Left.

Click.

CRASH!

The cage door burst open.

The hot, black mass knocked me to the ground.

Wind howled through the open door.

The Jaguar's cage was creaking, empty.

I stood shivering, mystified, and alone.

FINAL DAY

As you walk the grounds this morning greeting your new friends, accepting compliments from our cheerful staff, bearing witness to the peaceful splendor around you, take a moment and consider that tonight this will all be gone, living only in your memories.

Immerse yourself on this final day. Enjoy a special breakfast with your humble host, Ronan Rackham. He's handing out awards to the winners of the many parlor games held in the recreation room this week.

Special lectures will be held at various exhibits throughout the morning. Hear the inside scoop on your favorite animals from the men who spend their lives caring for them.

A valet will be sent to your room to assist you with packing. Our employees are always here to help.

You've faced many challenges on this adventure, but the hardest of all will be saying good-bye.

25.

I woke up with a knot in my stomach that day and knew exactly what to pin it on.

I'd been dreaming of the Jaguar's den. It was difficult to orient myself to my bedroom or even to remember walking back to my house.

I could only recall entering the front door and realizing I hadn't locked it when I left. *No robbers here,* I thought, *only mice.*

I laughed out loud and scared myself. I was sure to double-bolt the door.

I fell asleep the moment I got into bed, not realizing how tired I'd been.

And even though I had plenty to worry about, I felt a strange sense of peace.

It was over. Until the next day, at least.

And that's what the knot in my stomach was. The next day was here.

On the Golden Path near the bottom of the hill, Heppa and her son, Jarro, were talking to the lady with the red hat and a man who looked like her husband.

"You can have everything I've got on me now," the man bellowed, "and when we're back in Georgetown, we'll go to the bank and I'll give you more."

Heppa considered him sternly. The warm crinkles around her eyes were gone, no hint of a smile. She took Jarro by the arm and tried to walk around the couple, but the man stepped in front of them.

"I'll pay you a thousand pounds," he blurted out. "Two thousand! Just for a day!"

"We are not going back," Heppa said seriously.

"Please," said the lady in the red hat. "We can't find anyone to take us. We're very afraid. This is no place for people like us."

"I agree," Heppa said softly. "But here you are."

"Please!" the lady in the red hat begged. "You're supposed to help!"

"I am not your painting teacher now," Heppa said. "I don't want you to be hurt, but I will not put a *mishin* over my son."

Heppa's face crunched up like a fist. *Mishin* was the word our workers used for guests. It also means "dead fish."

"We are going alone," Heppa added with finality. "You stay until the boat comes—that is best. Do not bother anyone else. The jungle has a place for our people, but not for you."

The woman in the red hat looked shocked. She had probably never been denied by someone she thought inferior.

"If we stay here," her husband said cautiously, "how can we be safe? With the jaguar loose?"

Heppa sighed and shook her head. "Stay close to Ronan Rackham," she said, exchanging a glance with her son. "But not too close."

It was then that Jarro spotted me.

"Marlin! What are you doing here?"

I walked down to them and noticed that there were no guards posted on the walls. I searched the path on the pyramid for workers making rounds but saw no one.

"You should be with your father," Heppa said. "He should have sent someone for you." She waved away the anxious guests and ambled partway up the hill to me. She reached out and put her hands on my shoulders. "All of us are leaving. The jaguar escaped, and it's not safe for anyone."

Jarro touched her arm and said something in Arawak. Then he turned to me and said, "You should get inside." He adjusted the two cloth sacks draped over his shoulders, carrying what looked like all of their belongings. They really weren't coming back.

"Woo—wa—where?" I managed to ask.

"One of the villages, the other side of the river. We will

be safer there . . . ," Heppa said. "I don't know if they'd take you."

"The curse is on his family," said Jarro.

"That's what they'll think," Heppa replied.

"It's the truth!" Jarro said.

"I don't know," she whispered. "But Marlin, go to your father. Whatever your fate, it is tied with him."

She gave me a parting hug, but there was no comfort in it. I knew she was right.

26.

The path to Father's office was empty. No sweeping workers, no strolling guests. The administrative building was far from the pyramid, no animals nearby. Just the steady drone of the jungle.

Then a window shattered. Or a gun went off, it sounded like both. Glass exploded from a west-facing window, and I heard men shouting. I should have run away from there. Never in my life would I have gone toward the source of a gunshot.

But that was before.

In the reception room, it was quiet again. A large hardwood desk sat opposite the door. A guestbook lay open on the desk, flanked by two bronze sculptures: a chimpanzee in a ferocious pose and a sleeping jaguar. People always asked if we had a jaguar in the zoo when they signed the book. Father hated saying no.

I suppose it's no again.

Men were talking softly in Father's office. The door was ajar. RONAN RACKHAM, PROPRIETOR was written on its frosted glass.

I peeked round and felt my heart jump up into my throat. Father was backed against a desk with his hands at his sides. Leedo Flute was pointing a pistol at him.

I spun into the hallway and pressed myself to the wall. My mind flashed to Leedo saying Father might not come back from the hunt. He'd seemed to relish the thought. I'd never seen Father in danger like this before. I didn't know what to do.

"You give me what you owe me, and I will go," Leedo barked. Was he robbing Father?

"I'll give you your money," Father said. "But you've got to stay and help me. We need to find out who did this. And we need the men back at their posts."

Why would Father ask him to stay? The man was pointing a gun at him. I was in such shock at the sight that I struggled to understand what they were saying. I leaned closer to the doorframe and peeked one eye in at them.

"I won't do your dirty work anymore," Leedo said. He held the gun high, and it shook as he spoke.

Father was still calm. He put his hands out toward Leedo, though he kept his distance. "You're the only one I can trust with something like this. You and I have been through so much already, Leedo. We're in this together."

"I will not kill for you again."

I pulled back away from the doorframe, stifling a gasp. I felt light-headed. I gave myself a moment to put what Leedo had said together. But truthfully, I already understood.

"That won't be needed this time," Father said.

"This time will be worse," replied Leedo. "And you won't have the jaguar to blame it on."

I took a breath.

"I won't take another life," Leedo panted.

"You think I want it to be this way?" Father roared. "We have no choice. We must protect the zoo."

"There is no zoo. You destroyed it when you brought that jaguar here." I heard the gun's hammer click. "I will not give another warning."

"St—St—Stop!" I shouted, jumping into the doorway. Both men turned to me, startled, but stayed where they were: Leedo with the gun pointed at Father, and Father with his hands at his sides.

"Now your son knows what you've done," Leedo said. "Move!"

He pushed past Father and behind the desk to rifle through the drawers. I looked at Father, but his eyes wouldn't meet mine. He just stared at the floor between us. After a moment, he sat down on the corner of the desk.

Leedo found the drawer he was looking for and pulled out an envelope. He ripped off the flap and took out several dozen bank notes. He counted them and flung about half back on the desk.

177

"Only what I'm owed," he said to no one in particular. "I am no cheat."

Father was still at the desk, not looking at me.

I wanted to run away—not from Leedo and his gun, but from Father and whatever I was about to learn.

"Marlin," Leedo said, "you get out of here! This place is cursed. And you are cursed if you stay here with him," he added, pointing the gun at my father.

27.

"Wha—WHA—wha—whaaa—" My lips puckered, trying to speak.

Father still sat on the desk, frozen. Leedo was gone. We heard the door slam and stood there together, each waiting to see what the other would do.

"WH—WH—wha—WHA—"

I bit my lip. Father slowly perched himself on the edge of the desk, looking solemn. I started again.

"Wh—wh—wha—ah—aht d-d-did Le—le—le—leed—do—"

Father didn't help me finish. His mustache covered his tight lips.

Father was a liar. Rage urged me on. He was a murderer.

Lips, tongue, teeth, air.

"LEE—dd—DO mm—mmm—meee-aan," I forced myself to say. "A-a-a b-bout N—nnn—Nath-tam?"

Father got up from the edge of the desk and walked behind it. He eyed the money Leedo had thrown back on the table and swiped at it. Some of the notes fell into the desk drawer and some on the floor. Father ignored them. He drew out a pint of gin from the bottom of the drawer, unscrewed the cap, and took a swig.

"I said this was a lesson in management." He took another drink. "There are always hard decisions."

"Mum—m-murder?" I choked out.

"I protect this zoo!" Father slammed his palm on the desk. "My family. My employees. My animals."

He took a long drink, draining half the bottle.

"I protect it against men like the duke," Father said. "He's buying all the jungle he can, going to burn it down and raise sugarcane in the ashes."

Daddy's here to buy land for a sugar forest, Olivia had said in the carriage when we first met. *He says we might move here!*

"He'll destroy this place. Everything that makes it good, everything wild, will be gone. The animals, the people, burned up," Father said, tears ringing his eyes. "Who will come see us anymore, with the jungle gone and the whole interior a wasteland?"

Father's passion was real; he loved this place. But I couldn't forget.

"Wh—whh—whhhat ah-abah-about Nn—nn—"

"Nathtam," he said, taking another drink. "I've been fighting the duke at his own game for months. Snatching up the land before he can. But it's an expensive game, Marlin. I've put everything I have in it and borrowed the rest against the value of the zoo. If we miss a payment, the bank could take the zoo from us. The duke knows how thin I'm stretched, and that's why he hired Nathtam."

I blinked. What would the duke hire Nathtam for? Father was talking too fast. It didn't make sense.

"I made the Sky Shrine into a circus so I could charge the guests more. With more cash flow, I could keep buying land away from the duke. That's why he paid Nathtam to bring up this nonsense about the Sky Shrine being some sacred relic and duping the workers into a strike. We can't afford to get shut down for even a week. It was a terrible thing to have to do, Marlin. But if Nathtam had lived, the zoo would be lost and the jungle would burn." He looked at me with glistening eyes.

My mind was in revolt, trying to comprehend it all. Father was admitting that he'd ordered Leedo to murder Nathtam. More than that, he was telling me it was justified, that the zoo and the entire jungle were at risk of extinction.

The duke did seem to be trying to sabotage the zoo. When Tim was attacked, he turned it into a crusade to get refunds for all the guests. And when they'd first spoken to Father outside the gatehouse, the duchess had said that strange thing about being delighted we were still in business. Perhaps they had bribed Nathtam to strike.

But Father had killed him. Even if the zoo and the jungle hung in the balance, he was admitting that he'd killed Nathtam.

Questions battled each other in my mind, but it was so hard for me to speak. I had to choose carefully.

"J—ja—jaguar," I said.

"What?" Father's face screwed up in confusion. "Oh, yes. Well, we couldn't have the men thinking he'd been . . . so I had Leedo prepare the body. Make it look like a jaguar attack. Nathtam was gone, and I knew the men wouldn't stay in the jungle with a man-eater. They were still cross with me about the Sky Shrine, so I went out and caught a jaguar, claiming it was the killer. That way they could feel safe here again. They'd know I was the one who took care of them. I could protect them."

"Buh—buh—but," I stuttered. "Ah-ah li—lie."

Father looked at me sternly. "Not a lie, Marlin. A story. People tell each other stories every day. Who are we? What is our purpose? The duke paid Nathtam to convince our employees that the Sky Shrine was a sacred relic of their people. These are men who have worked on the pyramid for years. They've never cared about this pile of rock. It meant nothing to them. But they were won over by words.

"Remember this, Marlin: actions speak louder. I changed the story. I proved myself as Conqueror and Protector of this jungle."

There it was again, the phrase from the book. I'd never heard him say it before, but he said it with relish. "I proved it to the duke. I proved it to our guests. And I'll prove it to the world."

In the space of minutes he had moved from remorse to pride, and it enraged me that he would not stop talking. But still I pressed him—I couldn't help it.

"The j—j—j—j—JA-jaguar!" I shouted.

Father's eyes narrowed.

"The jaguar?" he said. "That bloody thing. I tried to do the best I could, but these natives. He inspired a madness in them." The corners of Father's mouth tightened, and his voice grew menacing. "I'll kill the savage who let him out."

I watched his mouth move as he spoke. The words were only sounds, I realized. Sounds I knew the meaning of, but they were of a language that was no longer my own.

Had never been my own.

"It Wa-WAH-Wah muh—muh—me," I said.

He couldn't understand me.

Lips, tongue, teeth, air.

"I wuh-WUH-was the wuh—one who la-luh—let the j-j—jag—wahr out," I said again.

My speech was imperfect as ever, but to drive home the meaning I had a secret weapon. I lifted the brass key out of my pocket and held it up for him to see.

He was silent. The only thing standing between me and his enormous frame was this little piece of metal. I squeezed it between my thumb and forefinger to keep it from shaking, and faintly, in the key's base, I could see my own reflection.

For once, I was the one wearing the Jungle Look.

I wanted to scream, but the stutter blocked my air. I grabbed the doorframe, but I feared that if I held on, I'd dislocate my shoulder.

He hadn't said anything to me. His face just gradually evolved from shock and doubt to rage. Then he came at me.

He took hold of my shirt like a crocodile, never letting go.

He pushed through the door to the outside and dragged me behind. I managed a stuttering call for help, but he clamped his other hand over my mouth.

We turned off the path and into the dense stand of awara trees. The sun peeked through the cracks in the canopy, and I watched the light skip over Father's face.

We were heading east. Our house was west of there, but we were headed toward the zoo.

He led me at arm's length, still gripping my shoulder, and we marched faster. We came through a thin stand of sand-box trees and emerged at the base of the pyramid opposite the Snake House. I struggled and yelped, but Father dragged me into the Snake House through the iron door.

It was cool and dark inside like always, the sounds of the resort muffled by thick walls. Father clamped onto me with both hands and drew me in front of him. I flinched and feared he'd hit me. "Both my sons have betrayed me," he growled, tears in his eyes. "You don't deserve the Rackham name."

Spittle sprayed my face and he shook me with each word. "D—dd—dd-don't ww—"

Don't want it, I tried to say, but he dug his fingers into my shoulders and shouted.

"Not another broken word."

He shoved me backward onto the stone, then turned on his heel and left through the iron door, slamming it behind him. I heard the key enter the lock and turn.

Now I was the one in a cage.

FINAL NIGHT

Night has fallen and you are safe in your beds, slowly rocking back and forth on the *Saint of the Animals* as it chugs along the river.

The Zoo at the Edge of the World is behind you, and memories of all you've seen dance merrily in your minds as you fill postcards with stories of Guiana. You came here as a traveler and leave as an adventurer, a Conqueror of the Jungle.

We hope you enjoyed your stay with us at the Zoo at the Edge of the World, and our founder and happy leader, Ronan Rackham, would like to leave you with a short poem he composed himself. Let it be a little lullaby to rock you to sleep.

Behold the fearless hunter as he treks along the path.
Alone he journeys forth into the jungle's holy wrath.
Behind him in the clearing is the village, meek and small.
For the safety of the villagers the hunter risks it all.

A whispering of leaves behind him lets the hunter know
A tiger is afoot! And swift the hunter draws his bow.
The villagers will feast tonight on golden tiger paws
That nearly caught the hunter's throat and stuffed him in its jaws.

28.

The empty capybara pen was made of thin metal rods. I unscrewed one of them from the frame and jammed it into the seam between the door and the wall. When I pulled, the rod bent. It was useless. Then I took the wooden stool from the staff room, raised it over my head, and brought it down on the brass door handle. I bashed it and the knob broke off, but the door still wouldn't open.

I didn't even know what I'd do if I got out. I wondered where the Jaguar was—long gone by now, I hoped. If I'd had it to do over again, I would have still freed him and still told Father I'd done it. But there was no way I would have stuck around for his reaction.

Father wasn't the man I thought he was. He loved the jungle, and what the duke had planned was terrible, but I couldn't comprehend what Father had done to Nathtam.

The thought of it hit me hard every time I allowed it in. My father had killed a man—or ordered a man killed, which was no different.

And that made him a murderer. I'd always been frightened of that word and what it meant. It was a word beyond reason, living in shadows. But if I stayed in the light, I always thought, I'd be safe. Father didn't live in the shadows. He wasn't insane. He was a reasonable man, yet now he said he had reasons to be a murderer.

Night fell and the moonlight came through the windows at the top of the Snake House. They were open but too high for me to reach, even standing on the stool.

The snakes and frogs and lizards in their cases were quiet and still. I put my mouth to the glass and tried to talk, but they didn't answer.

Dead Eyes was there, just as quiet and motionless as the rest of them. The hills and valleys of his enormous body filled his cramped case in a messy heap. I tried to follow his body from head to tail, but I couldn't unravel him.

The *BANG* of a gunshot rang through the window at the top of the Snake House. The second gunshot I'd heard that day.

Faint sounds I couldn't make out came through in tiny peeps.

Screams. Far away, but they were human.

I ran to the door and tried to open it again. But the knob was busted, and the door was still locked.

The screams were louder now. I could make out a woman's voice, shrill and howling.

I picked up the stool and bashed its leg into the dent where the knob was, trying to bust through the lock. I rushed at it from the other side of the room and hit the door like a battering ram.

The stool leg cracked, and the seat hit my chest and knocked the wind out of me. The door didn't budge.

BANG!

Another gun blast sounded.

The screams through the window were shriller now. I pounded my fists on the heavy door.

No one answered.

"Master Marlin!"

A voice called from far away. I shot up from the stone floor where I'd crouched, my ear perked to the window.

"Master Marlin!" the voice rang out again. It was Kenji.

"Kenji! Kenji!" I screamed desperately. My fingers pressed against the rough brick of the walls, lifting me slightly higher so that I might catch a sound.

"Master Marlin!" Kenji appeared in the window above. I leaped back and pumped my fist in the air.

"Boy, am I glad to see you!" I said.

"Master Marlin, what are you doing in here?"

"Father locked me up," I said. "He was the one who killed Nathtam."

"What?" Kenji said, climbing down the wall and hanging off the bricks.

"It doesn't matter, Kenj," I said. "What's going on?"

"The jaguar stole the keys and gave them to the apes."

"What?"

"Master Marlin let him out of the cage," Kenji said. "That was very bad."

"But . . . Father was going to kill him."

"And now he's going to kill your father," she said. "He snuck into your house at night and snatched the keys. He brought them to Monkey Maze and said, 'You with hands, split these up and let out the animals. Tonight, we take the jungle back.'"

That explained the shooting, and the screaming.

"Was anyone hurt?" I asked. "Were any animals shot?"

"There was no one left to do any shooting. All the guards ran away."

"I heard a gun go off."

"Your father got a gun. But the chimpanzees took it."

"Is he all right?" I asked.

"All the people are heading for the Great Hall. They're scared." She reached for my collar and pulled herself off the wall and onto my shoulder. "Kenji's scared too."

A shadow fell over us.

I looked up to the window and saw the moonlight blocked by a furry silhouette. The muscled mass squeezed its way through the small opening and spilled out onto the ledge above. We retreated to the other side of the room, and I took the stool in my hand again.

"There's going to be another circus show," said the shadow. "And this time, little Marlin, you're the star."

Blue Boy the chimp was standing before us. His lips curled in a devious smile, and he stank of filth. His arm extended powerfully and dangled a small set of brass keys.

"Did you lose these? Or was that your father?" The chimp laughed. "You all look the same to me."

I could tell from the shape of the ring that these were keys to the cages on the eastern side of the zoo. The Snake House key would be on that chain.

"I've been trying to find this little one, Kenji," Blue Boy said. "Glad I thought to follow you!"

"Puh—Please," I said, "let me go. I can lead the people out of here. They'll never come to the jungle again."

"You can trust Master Marlin!" Kenji pleaded.

Blue Boy gave Kenji a withering look. "I did trust 'Master Marlin' once, and he made me jaguar bait."

"I'm sorry," I pleaded. "That was a mistake! I didn't think he would—"

"Stay away from him!" Kenji shrieked, jumping between me and the chimp.

"I'm returning the favor," he grunted, kicking Kenji into the wall. She crumpled to the ground.

"Please don't—" I backed into a row of display cases.

"Now, now, I'm not going to hurt you," Blue Boy said,

and his eyes shone. "But I can't speak for him."

He gestured to the back of the Snake House, where Dead Eyes lay dormant behind his triple-thick glass.

The chimpanzee padded over and rapped loudly with his knuckles.

"You awake in there?"

He considered the keys on the chain and glanced at the lock below Dead Eyes's feeding chute. He tried to shove a key into the hole, but it was too big. He tried another that fitted but wouldn't turn. Then another and another, methodically.

I knew which was the right key, and when he slid it into the lock, I couldn't help screaming.

"Don't!" I yelled. "The Jaguar and I—we're friends. If I get killed, he'd—"

"What the jaguar doesn't know won't hurt him." He laughed. With a flick of Blue Boy's wrist, the key released the latch, and the triple-thick glass of Dead Eyes's exhibit slowly, creakily swung open.

Moonlight filtered through and illuminated the terrible snake in all his greatness.

Blue Boy jumped up and down excitedly.

"And now the real show begins!"

I felt my muscles seize in horror, my body rigid with fear. I was fifteen feet away from a monster that could kill me in an instant.

"Take him, snake!" Blue Boy called. "Feed!"

The moonlight seemed to change from blue to yellow.

Or no, it wasn't the moon. It was the snake. He'd shot across the room and filled my vision with his swirling skin.

But he hadn't come for me.

Choking screams issued from the center of a tornado that his body had made. At the peak, I saw Blue Boy, gasping with his arms in agony, caught up in a death grip. The snake undulated up and down with the struggling chimp, wrapping his body around him, constricting.

I turned away and saw a glint of golden light. The keys had flown from Blue Boy's grip and clinked down at my feet. Kenji was reviving herself and climbing the bricks toward the window ledge. I picked up the keys and turned to the door.

The knob was smashed off, but the mechanism was broken only here on the inside. The door could still be unlocked from the exterior.

Blue Boy thrashed and gurgled as the snake lifted him higher.

I called to Kenji at the window. "Take these and let me out on the other side of the door." I threw her the keys and she caught them without looking, fixated on Blue Boy's death rattle.

"Kenji, now!"

She pulled her eyes away from the horror and looked down at the keys.

"Kenji isn't strong enough to turn the lock!" she said.

"You have to try!" I shouted.

"Not strong enough!" she called, looking at Blue Boy as he went limp. "Kenji must go!"

"No!" I screamed as she leaped into the night. "Kenji, come back! Kenji—"

I froze midsentence. It was silent in the Snake House. Kenji was gone, and Blue Boy was no more.

It was only me and Dead Eyes now.

And, for me, Dead Eyes listened.

29.

I tried not to look, but I couldn't turn my back on Dead Eyes either, so I ended up watching him swallow Blue Boy whole. There was almost no noise. Dead Eyes slowly loosened his jaw away from his skull and slid his mouth and face around the chimp like a sock sliding up a foot.

"This is the hardest part," Dead Eyes said around Blue Boy's body. "My throat has become a bit sensitive in my old age."

I didn't respond. The old blind snake bobbed his head back and forth slightly above the floor. It was the first time I'd ever gotten a good look at his face.

Black, pebbled skin radiated from his sharp snout, and small shadings of yellow and orange lurked between the scales. When he spoke, I could see the double rows of sharp teeth, one following the line of his lips like most animals', and one leading down his throat.

His eyes were withered and gray, lacking the strange glow most snakes' eyes had. They'd been scratched out years ago and were dead things now.

He was silent and listened for me to respond.

"You don't need to be afraid of me, Marlin. I do not care about a jaguar, nor your father."

Again, I didn't respond. Without moving my shoulders, I craned my neck toward the staff room in the back of the Snake House. If the door was open, I could race there and slam it shut behind me. *Someone will come for me eventually,* I thought. *Unless everyone forgot about me and ran off. Then I'll starve there. But I'd rather starve than be snake food.*

My neck muscles strained as I flexed them to their limits. I stared and squinted. The door was closed. I'd slammed it shut when I'd dragged the stool out.

Dead Eyes would be slowed by the meal still in him. If I made a straight run for the staff room, I could unlock the door and close it before he caught me.

But I'd need the keys for that. And I'd given those to Kenji, who'd run away with them.

For a moment, I cursed Kenji for abandoning me. But I couldn't blame her. This was my fault.

"Are you thinking that I'll eat you, Marlin?" Dead Eyes laughed. "But I am so full."

His tail began to writhe and twist. Between his head and the lump in his neck, the snake was immobile. But the length of his body behind the digesting meal was still active and deadly.

"It seems as though the zoo is under new management," he hissed. "I wonder if the monkeys will come to feed me after what I've done to their friend."

Dead Eyes flexed his neck horribly and moved the Blue Boy—shaped lump farther down his body.

"It doesn't matter," he went on. "This meal will last some weeks. And until then, well, I'm lucky to have you here, Marlin. You may keep me company."

His back end slid toward me across the floor like a whip. I pushed against the top of a display case and lifted my feet as the tail swished under me. Silently, I touched the ground, toes first.

"I just want to get a grip on you, Marlin." The snake heaved, growing angry. "You know I like a live feeding."

Again, he swept the floor with his enormous body. He could have cleared the whole length of the Snake House if it hadn't been for the lump anchoring his neck. But he'd find me soon enough.

The thick, black body came sliding toward me. It was too fast this time, and I was forced to leap onto the display case, breaking through the glass lid. My hand squished into a lizard's food bowl, and the little creature nipped at my thumb. I yanked my arm out of the case and cut it on the broken glass.

"There you are!" Dead Eyes shouted, and flung the whole

 197

weight of his back half against me. It knocked me over to the shelf of lizard displays on the opposite side. The small end of his tail hung over the glass and draped down my shoulder. It sensed me immediately and curled around my neck.

I forced my fingers between my skin and his. I could feel the jerk of his body on the other side of the display shelf, trying to move the bulk of his body toward me, weighed down by the chimpanzee inside his throat.

I managed to get my fingers around his tail, and with all my strength, I was able to uncurl it.

The small end of the tail grasped for me like an arm, and the thicker parts down his body flexed and bent and dragged his top half nearer.

His midsection rose above me, thick as a tree trunk, and came down with all its weight, crushing me beneath it. I could not lift him off or roll away. He grew heavier on top of me.

"Marlin!"

A girl's voice screamed as the great iron door to the Snake House opened.

Dead Eyes's midsection tensed and slid away, launching toward the door.

"Ol—Olivia!" I shouted.

She stood there in the doorway, Kenji perched on her shoulder. She was in shock and stiffly held the key to the Snake House in her hand.

"Who's there?" Dead Eyes bellowed. He whipped all his

weight toward the intruders, sliding toward the door where Olivia remained frozen.

I jumped to my feet, sprinted five paces toward Dead Eyes, and kicked him full force in the face. His head reeled back from the blow, and his jaw flailed horribly.

I leaped over three or four layers of writhing flesh and tackled Olivia, gripping the unbroken exterior handle and pulling it shut behind me.

Behind it, Dead Eyes screamed.

30.

"That was a snake," Olivia said in shock.

We'd landed on the grimy stones, and she was underneath me. Her face was red and dusted with dirt. Little streams of clean skin descended from her eyes where she'd been crying. I shuffled off her and pulled us both up to sitting. She looked disoriented and had trouble focusing on me.

"AAh-AAH-O—livi—a," I stammered, putting my hands on her shoulders. She turned to me and her mouth opened in a soft shape, but she didn't say anything. She looked at me, uncertain.

I hugged her and she sighed. "Ehh—It's ah—okay," I said. "Okay." Her arms came around my back and pulled me tighter to her. I regretted acting angry with her the night before. Both of our fathers had done terrible things, and she couldn't change what hers had done any more than I could mine.

"It's scary out here, Marlin," she said with her chin on my

shoulder. "The animals broke their cages."

"Ah—I ne—ne—know," I said.

"What were you doing locked in there?" Olivia asked, pulling away. "That thing could have killed you."

"Ma—My ffff—father." I lowered my head.

"He put you in there?" Olivia asked. "I don't understand, Marlin. Why would he do that?"

I couldn't answer her.

"My mother and father are missing," she said. "Everyone went to the Great Hall to hide, but my parents never arrived. So I left to look for them. Kenji came up to me with these keys, and she started pulling at me and screeching and led me here. How did she know you were in trouble?"

I turned to Kenji and put out my hand. She scampered over and scaled my arm to my shoulder. I kissed her on the cheek and said, "Thank you, my friend."

"Of course!" Kenji shrieked. "Kenji went to get help. What did you think I was doing?"

"Getting help, of course." I laughed. "I knew you wouldn't leave me."

"Yeah, you better know that!"

Olivia looked at Kenji and me. "What are you doing?"

"Uh . . ." I turned back to her. "N—n—nnn—nothing."

"We should really go, Master Marlin," Kenji whispered to me. "Chimps are prowling."

I nodded and helped Olivia to her feet. "Guh-Guh—Great Hall," I managed, and tried to pull Olivia westward, but she pulled back.

"Marlin, I have to find my parents." She was scared, but the fight hadn't left her. She wouldn't leave without them, and I wouldn't leave without her.

"Ah—ah—okay," I said. So we turned south, up the Golden Path, into the zoo.

31.

The spectacled bear cage was open and empty, with no sign of where Mala and Bashtee had gone. Likewise in the Boar Den—Tuskus, Gray Beard, and Belly Wart were gone, and the door to the pen was swinging in the wind. But the bush dogs exhibit was untouched. All five dogs howled at me. "Let us out! Let us out, too!"

The gate to the Tapir Pond was still bolted, and Bottleby and Longsnout half hid themselves in the water. There seemed to be no logic to it.

"Ahoy, down there, Marlin!" came calls from above our heads. I looked up to see Eddo and Bill, the two toucans, circling my head along with Tappet, the bird of paradise.

"Be careful there, Marlin!" Tappet chirped.

Olivia was looking up at the squawking birds as well. She already seemed a little scared of the attention they were giving us, and I couldn't blame her with the state the zoo was in.

"Hey you guys, come down here!" Kenji hooted, throwing her hands in the air. "Master Marlin needs your help!"

The three birds spiraled down through the air and landed on the ground in front of us. Olivia jumped back at the strange sight as Tappet and Eddo hopped forward. "What can we do for you, Marlin?"

"Yes," Bill echoed. "We owe you one after you helped out with him." He cocked his head toward Tappet.

"Helping out with who?" Tappet demanded, jumping up and down.

"No one!" Eddo said.

"No one!" Bill agreed.

I didn't want to frighten Olivia further by chatting with the birds right in front of her, but there were chimps on the loose, and I didn't know what else to do. All our animals could be dangerous when panicked, and panic was ruling the day. Explaining myself to Olivia would have to come second.

"We're looking for some people," I said.

"People? We've seen people everywhere," Eddo said.

"They've been making a racket worse than him," Bill said.

"Worse than who?" Tappet squawked.

"No one!" said Eddo.

"No one!" Bill repeated.

"Listen to me!" I shouted at them. "I'm looking for a man and a woman. The man is big, with a pointy silver beard. The woman . . . well she looks like her, but taller." I turned around and pointed at Olivia. I don't know what kind of a madman I must have seemed to her, but I didn't care.

"You sure that's not her, right there?" Tappet asked.

"Yes, I am," I said. "But she looks like her."

"Hmmm . . . ," said Eddo, turning to Bill.

"Hmmm . . . ," Bill responded.

"Sorry, but no!" they both said together.

I stood up and looked at Kenji, shaking my head. "Marlin?" Olivia asked me delicately. "What are you doing with those birds?"

Before I could begin to summon up an answer, a trumpet call cut through the night. It was accompanied by the stomping of feet on stone that grew louder and nearer from behind a stand of trees.

"What's that?" asked Eddo.

"What's that?" Bill echoed him.

"That's an elephant, I think," said Tappet.

"An elephant?" Bill and Eddo repeated, jumping into the air.

The birch trees lining the path next to the empty Boar Den burst into splinters. Dreyfus smashed through them in a frenzied gallop. He barreled down the path toward where we were standing, rattling the stones underneath him with every thundering step.

He trumpeted in panic and shook his wide gray head. A flaming torch was tied to the end of his trunk, swinging side to side and setting trees aflame.

Olivia screamed as he charged us, and Kenji scaled my back and wrapped her paws around my neck. Bill, Eddo, and Tappet scattered in all directions. Dreyfus galloped right at us, and Olivia tried to pull me off the path, but I pushed her away. "G—go!" I said.

Dreyfus broke his stride within inches of me and reared up, kicking his forelegs in the air as smoke streamed from his trunk.

"Dreyfus!" I shouted. "Stop!" His dirty toe caught me in the chin and knocked me back onto the path. He was standing at his full height above me, and a tower of smoke extended to the sky. He looked like an enormous puppet being held up by a string. When he came down, I had to roll between the wrinkled pillars of his legs to avoid getting smashed.

"Tim's trick!" I called to him, remembering the circus bit they'd performed. "Let me up!"

Dreyfus bent his knee and lowered his head. "Marlin, help me," he gasped.

The burning torch was under his face, and hot smoke burned his eyes. I climbed his knee and grabbed hold of his tusk. A smoldering piece of ash touched his skin, and he reared back in pain, nearly tossing me.

I lifted my stomach onto his tusk and put a foot in his open mouth to hoist myself over his head. When I was up, I lay flat on my tummy between his eyes and secured my feet in the crooks of his ears.

"Take it off!" he moaned as the torch shifted up his trunk. It'd been lashed there with a length of hemp and was now riding up the trunk.

I unhooked my toes from the crooks of his ears and took a bumpy ride down to the end of his trunk. Smoke was streaming into my eyes now, and I had to reach around the flame to feel the strands of hemp wrapped round each other. The heat hurt my face, and my right palm was screaming with pain. Still, I probed behind the torch with my hands while my legs were wrapped around his trunk, my feet in his mouth. I tried to lift the torch away from his skin but couldn't find a loose end in the hemp. Still, I sensed it had some give.

Desperate, I pulled the torch farther up his trunk and let it fall on Dreyfus's skin.

He shrieked, but it gave me the slack I needed to pull the tangle of hemp onto the fire. It crackled and in an instant burned away, dropping the torch and me to the Golden Path below.

I fell on my back as Olivia stamped out the flames with her boot sole. She pulled me up, and my vision was spinning slightly. All the trees along the Golden Path were now raging with fire. Red smoke clouds formed in the sky.

Dreyfus collapsed and extended his trunk to me.

"What happened to you?" I gasped.

"The apes," he moaned. "They opened my gate, and when I wouldn't go with them, they tied the torch to me and lit it."

I clamped my aching right palm beneath my armpit and leaned against him. "You have to get out of here," I said. "The apes have gone mad. It isn't safe."

Dreyfus blinked the smoke out of his teary eyes. I saw the sensitive skin on his trunk turning red and was relieved I'd gotten the torch off before the burn was too serious. His skin hadn't made contact with the flames for long. It was mostly the smoke and the heat that had panicked him.

"Marlin!" a voice called from the air. I looked up. It was Tappet. "I've found them! I've found the woman and the man!"

"I have to go now," I said to Dreyfus, gently stroking his snout. "Promise me you'll get somewhere safe."

"I will," the elephant said, getting up and shaking out his ears. "But where are you going?"

I turned to Olivia, who was now standing at my side, shaking. I took her by the hand and said in the animal tongue, "We have people to find."

32.

We trailed after Tappet at a sprint, breaking off the Golden Path and dodging between buildings and exhibits. The destruction Dreyfus had wrought was everywhere: smashed trees and fences, fires spreading through broken branches and wooden structures. I was thankful that our animal exhibits were all metal and stone and wouldn't burn, but the trees and fences all around gave off a monstrous heat and plumes of smoke that drove the animals still trapped in the cages mad with fear. They called for me to help them, but Father had taken my keys when he'd locked me in the Snake House.

We followed Tappet down the pyramid to a heavily wooded park at the base, which was dominated by fifty-foot-tall bitter berry trees. The shrubs at the edges of the park had caught fire, and the wind whipped the flames high. We heard a moaning growl and human screams from within the park.

Tappet chirped, "In there!"

Olivia saw them first. "Mum! Dad!" she shouted, and took off. Kenji and I followed her, trying to see where she was headed, but we were too far behind. A roar sounded, and Mala, our two-hundred-pound spectacled bear, appeared before Olivia and swiped at her. Olivia stopped short in time and dodged it. That's when I saw them. The duke and the duchess were partway up a tree, clinging to the branches for dear life.

"Olivia!" the duke bellowed.

"Darling!" cried the duchess.

She scrambled away from the bear and back toward me. Mala charged her for a few paces and roared. Spectacled bears are mostly vegetarians and wouldn't think of hurting a human even if they were starving. But Mala foamed and roared and reared up on her hind legs. When Olivia was far enough back, she turned around and refocused herself on the tree the duke and duchess were in. Mala screamed, "Get away from him!" and leaped up on the trunk. She tried to climb to where the duke and duchess were cowering, but all around the base of the tree were stumps from broken branches, and the bear couldn't get a foothold.

"Run away, Olivia!" the duchess screamed.

"Go!" called the duke.

Mala roared and clawed at the base of the tree. "You get away from him!" she bellowed. She leaped up against the trunk and gained traction with her claws, snapping at the duchess's feet and pulling off a white leather boot.

"Mala, stop!" I shouted, coming up behind her.

She turned to me and snarled. "Leave me alone, Marlin!"

"Where is Bashtee?" I called to her.

"What are you doing, boy?" the duke shouted at me. "Get Olivia out of here!"

"Bring help!" the duchess shrieked.

I went up closer to the tree. The flame from the shrubs had caught onto the bitter berry trees at the edges, and the smoke was clouding the treetops.

"Is Bashtee up there?" I said to Mala as she chomped at a branch below the duchess's feet.

"The boy is mad," the duchess cried. "Olivia, you must run!"

I heard twigs cracking behind me and then Olivia was at my side, Kenji perched on her shoulder. "Marlin will help you, Mother," she said. "You need to trust him!"

I turned to look at her. She didn't think I was crazy.

"Please, Marlin," she begged me.

I nodded and ran to the base of the tree below the bear. "Is Bashtee up there?" I called to Mala, who had climbed up a few feet above my head. She looked down at me and roared, "Go away!" I couldn't see the top of the tree because of all the smoke, but I knew the only thing that would drive her to this. I grabbed hold of the broken stub of a branch and pulled myself up onto the trunk. There was splintered wood everywhere, but the tree was sticky with sap, and it made my grip stronger. I pulled myself higher until my head was at Mala's belly. When I reached the level of her face, she snapped at me.

"Marlin, stay away from him!" Her jaws clamped on a branch where my hand had just been. She clawed at me and tore the shoulder of my shirt, drawing blood.

"I will not hurt Bashtee!" I screamed at her. "When you thought he was lost, that he wasn't your cub, I found him for you. I brought him back for you."

The bear's face contorted for an instant in recognition. It was the second I needed to grab hold of the duchess's bare foot and pull myself up to a higher branch.

"Oh!" she screamed, kicking at me with her other heel.

Mala's mothering instinct overpowered her again and she swiped at me, barely missing my guts.

"Help him up, Mother!" Olivia screamed furiously from below. The duke grabbed hold of my collar and hoisted me up to the branch where they were teetering.

He lost his balance, and I grabbed his belt. For a moment, I entertained the thought of letting go. It would be a better world if Guiana had one less ravisher. He looked at me fearfully and flailed for support. His fate was in my hands. The animals would be saved, the jungle preserved, and my father avenged.

And, like my father, I would be a murderer.

I pulled the duke back toward the safety of the tree trunk and grabbed the branch above me. I hoisted myself up above the Duke and Duchess of Bradshire but made sure to put a foot on each of their heads for a boost.

"Ow! Watch it!" they cried, and I ascended, smiling.

High up in the tree, through the haze of the smoke, I saw Bashtee. He had climbed far up into the tree to get away from whatever had scared him, but he let me lift him off the branch and tuck him under one arm.

The Bradshires made for excellent ladders on my way down. My boots marked their white clothing brilliantly.

"My baby!" Mala moaned as I handed Bashtee down to her, setting the cub gently on her head. She dropped off the trunk of the tree, picked Bashtee up by the nape of his neck, and trotted off with him through the trees and away from the fire.

The duke and duchess slid to the ground, much less gracefully, and Olivia ran to them. The family pulled together, all crying with relief. Kenji and I surveyed the scene from a respectful distance, but I did overhear Olivia comforting her mother.

"It's all right," she said. "We're with Marlin now."

33.

I pressed the duke and duchess to move toward the Great Hall quickly, though they had both been badly shaken. "C—cc—cuh—cu—come on!" I scolded them, and for once they did not smirk at my stutter.

I had to find my father. The fires were getting worse, and the animals still in their cages were terrified. There was no choice now but to let them all out, but he had the keys.

We reached the Great Hall and found the enormous double door barricaded, but not locked, which gave me a sick feeling. It meant no one inside had a key to the door, so my father was not there. I banged on the door and heard screams from within, but it didn't open. The duke strode up beside and called, "It is I, the Duke of Bradshire and my family." He gave me a quick look. "And Marlin Rackham!" he added.

We heard what sounded like the movement of heavy

furniture, and the portal opened. The Great Hall was a mess. Chairs and tables had been turned over and piled by all the doors and windows. A shocked-looking young man greeted us.

"Hello, my lord," he said. "Please come in quickly!"

I surveyed the gathering of terrified guests and confirmed that my father was not among them. Nor were there any workers; they must have all abandoned the zoo that morning. It was a sad-looking lot. Families were huddled together and fearful. The lady in the red hat was there with her husband. "Close the door!" she demanded.

The young man who had opened it for us swung it shut and moved to push a broken table in front of it again. I touched his arm to stop him.

"Marlin, what are you doing?" Olivia asked me, but I sensed she already knew.

"The bub—bb-b-b-boat . . . ," I said to her, drawing her close to me.

"Yes, your father said it would come soon," she agreed. "But you need to wait here with us."

I shook my head. "I mm-mm-must f-find him."

"You don't even know where to look! He could be anywhere. Just stay until the boat comes."

"Kenji," I called to the little monkey. "Come on!" She hopped onto my shoulder.

Olivia grabbed my torn shirt sleeve. "Does anyone know where Captain Rackham is?" she called to the group.

"I saw him," said the young man who had let us in through the door.

"Wuh—WH-ww-where?" I spit out.

"He found me in a patch of brush along the path," the man said. "He told me I needed to follow him. We ran to a shed he said had guns in it. But before we got to the door, a group of chimps attacked. They threw me down." The man showed me a gash on his forehead. "When I came to, they were far away, dragging him up the steps."

I locked eyes with Olivia.

"Up?" she said.

I threw a broken table out of the way and marched out the door.

"Marlin, wait!" she cried, and followed me onto the path. "You can't go up there." She grabbed my arm and pulled me back toward the door. I tried to shake her loose, but she dug in her heels and held firm.

"B—buh—buh-bar the dd—d—door."

"No!" She shook her head and said, "Stay here."

She pulled me off-balance and I fell into her arms. She clung to me.

"There's something wonderful about you," she said. "I knew it when we first met." She gripped me tightly. "You must promise me you'll be all right."

"Ah-a—aa—I will," I managed, pushing away from her.

She grabbed my collar and drew me close again. Our noses touched and her breath was warm on my face. When she closed her eyes, tears streamed out and she kissed me.

I stood there motionless and heat spread across my cheeks. The little hairs stood up on the back of my head.

"Wow!" Kenji gasped. She was still on my shoulder, her face inches from ours.

"Kenji!" Olivia laughed and covered her mouth with her hand. I laughed too.

"I will see you soon," she said determinedly.

I nodded.

"Be safe, Marlin."

I reassured her with one last glance, and she retreated back into the Great Hall, closing the door. I heard furniture screeching along the floor to bar it.

Kenji and I left for the Golden Path. I knew where to find Father and the Jaguar.

I was still a Rackham.

Even if I didn't know what that meant anymore.

34.

My knees cracked and popped as we climbed the steps of the pyramid up to the Sky Shrine. My head was light. The smoke from burning trees rose up the pyramid in a fog of ash. My eyes watered and my throat was dry. But I did not feel any pain.

Kenji coughed and wheezed. "Kenji can't breathe!" she cried out near the top. I suspected she was overcome half by the smoke and half by the fear of what was waiting.

A gunshot rang out over the cackles of apes.

"You go back, Kenj." I knelt next to her on the step. "You've helped me enough, I think."

Kenji looked down. "Why don't you come back too?"

"Because this is my fault."

A waft of smoke blew into Kenji's eyes and she winced. She was such a small creature.

"I'm sorry, friend." I held out my hand. She crept into my

arms. I held her there for a moment and closed my eyes. In my mind, I returned to the corner behind my bed where I'd whispered to her. We were so far from that place now, but that's where all this had begun. And here was the end of it.

"I love you, Kenj," I whispered into the fur on the top of her head. "And I want you to go back."

"Okay, Master Marlin," Kenji chirped, and gave me one last squeeze.

She dropped from my arms to the steps below and hopped down them one by one. The smoke was thickening around the pyramid like a cloud, and after a dozen steps, I couldn't see her anymore.

She disappeared, and I kept climbing.

I couldn't see two yards in front of me, but I could tell from the smooth stones beneath my soles that I had reached the peak. It was five paces to the brick stairs leading down into the bowl of the Sky Shrine.

A few steps down and the air cleared. The smoke, lighter than air, still rose up the walls of the pyramid, but didn't sink into the pit. It was like being in a bubble, trapped underwater. The canvas tent was burned away because of my previous visit, but the smoke made its own black ceiling and blotted out the stars. Only a bit of moonlight shone through.

I made out the shapes of chimpanzees roiling in the bleachers. They were hooting at the action down below. I crouched and crept toward the pit.

A gunshot popped and all the chimps went mad laughing. Screecher rose above them all, gripping a rifle. He banged the butt of it on the stone and it went off.

The flash from the muzzle cast light on the pit. And I saw my father down there.

With the Jaguar.

From where I was, they both looked small. The Jaguar stalked my father, who retreated. Without thinking, I was at a run, bounding down the steps of the bleachers toward the pit. The apes' fur and filth brushed against me as I ran. I leaped off the edge toward my father and the Jaguar.

Then I was in the dust of the pit.

The Jaguar's teeth caught the moonlight. They got bigger as he approached me.

"Marlin," he purred. To his cat eyes, I was clear as day.

I could hear Father's heavy breathing off to my right. A brief opening in the smoke ceiling shed some light, and I saw him collapsed in the center of the pit.

He was the ringmaster there two days ago.

He glanced up in a panic and saw me, the Jungle Look stretched across his face. He stumbled toward me, tripping over his torn-up boots.

"Marlin," he gasped, though it was barely a word.

Both my father and the Jaguar approached, but Father caught me first. His thick, hairy arm scooped me up. I felt both embraced and ensnared. He held me close, pressed against his chest, the Jaguar several paces away.

"We have to stay together," he whispered.

I struggled in his grip. My arm was clamped awkwardly against my face, and I could smell his awful breath and feel his ragged heartbeat.

"La-le—laa—let g-gg—ah—go!" I stammered. This isn't how I wanted things to be. I'd come to save him.

The Jaguar stopped a few feet in front of us, looking amused.

"Marlin," Father gasped. "We'll get past him, make it out the big doors." He stared straight ahead at the Jaguar.

"L—l—listen!" I cried, struggling. But he wouldn't let go. He started to back away toward the doors, dragging me by my feet. He was stronger than me and he wouldn't stop.

"Nnn-NN—no!" I reared back my head and knocked him in the nose. I felt it crack against the back of my skull. His grip came apart and he covered his face. I managed to escape him and ran toward the Jaguar. Behind me he tried to choke out a warning but could make only a gurgling grunt.

"What are you doing?" I accosted the Jaguar. My face was flushed from my struggle with Father, and blood rushed through my body. I was shaking.

The beast considered me as coolly as ever, but beneath his expression I could sense unease.

"I'm doing the same as your father has done all these years," the Jaguar pronounced. "Whatever pleases me."

"And that means torturing him?" I said, stepping up, face-to-face, inches from his snout. "You going to kill him too?

You and these mad apes!"

The chimps, whose night vision was as bad as mine, must have recognized me then. I heard them hoot and shout, but I didn't care. They rushed up to the inward edge of the bleachers, enjoying the show. But I stayed focused on the Jaguar.

"I do what I believe to be right," the Jaguar said, heat entering his voice. "This is punishment."

"I thought there was no punishment in the jungle," I barked. "I thought there was no revenge, no torture."

"There's no law in the jungle," the Jaguar growled. "And above all, no creatures lording their laws above others."

"Then what do you call this?" I said, "These apes made war on the zoo. They're burning it to the ground."

"I'm not responsible for what they do."

"You are—when you let someone out of a cage, you are responsible." Every night he'd lectured me on the ways of the world, and I'd listened to him. But now he was wrong.

The Jaguar laughed. "Is that why you've come here?"

"Among other reasons. Why do you have my father?"

The Jaguar didn't answer. He only blinked.

"To kill him?" I said. "I won't let you."

A twitch sparked across the Jaguar's face. His muzzle dropped an inch.

222

"After everything you've seen," he said, voice low, "you side with him?"

I looked at Father. He'd pressed himself against the walls

of the pit, clutching his nose. The filthy apes jeered at him from above, the zoo in flames behind them. Screecher dangled the gun over Father's head, laughing.

"There are no sides in this, Jaguar," I said, turning back. "I don't know what kind of a man my father is, but he is my father and that will not change. I will protect him."

"We kill man or they kill us," said the Jaguar, growing agitated. "Look around! That is the way."

"I am a man," I said. "Do you kill me?"

"You are not a man," the Jaguar answered.

"I am."

"You are like me." The Jaguar growled. He breathed heavily through his teeth.

"Maybe I am," I said. "But I'll still protect him. The same as I would you."

The Jaguar's eyes widened in horror. His lips pulled back and showed his teeth. Behind me, I heard a shot and a scream.

Father had wrestled the gun from Screecher and fired into the chimp horde. They scattered up the benches of the Sky Shrine in all directions.

"Move, boy!" Father shouted—the barrel of the gun pointed toward the Jaguar beside me.

"Nn—NN—NO!" I screamed. But the Jaguar tossed me aside with his powerful head and I fell on my back in the dust. With every desire I willed myself to leap up, but my body would not respond. I heaved helplessly for breath. The

Jaguar crouched down in anticipation and quaked suddenly.

I didn't hear the gunshot. I only saw the Jaguar's fore-legs tense together and his haunches shift uselessly. A great exhalation of breath issued from his snout, and the Jaguar slumped to the ground.

Then I heard it.

My eyes were torn away from my friend as I was hauled up onto Father's shoulder. I cried incoherently, kicking and writhing, but he gripped me tight.

"Be still!" he commanded, brandishing the gun in one hand. "There are no more bullets. We have to go."

I grabbed his hair and pulled with all my strength. I kicked at his stomach and his arm holding the gun and bashed my palm into his broken nose. He gasped and dropped me to the ground.

"Marlin!" he commanded, but I scrambled away from him. The apes had regained their courage and were drop-ping down the walls into the pit. Trébone led their charge to the center, "He has killed the jaguar!" he shouted.

I ran to meet the apes as they circled his body. The Jag-uar lay there in the dust, struggling to breathe.

"Marlin!" Father called to me. "Come now!" I turned to him and saw that he didn't dare come any nearer to the angry horde of chimps that surrounded me. "I won't leave without you!"

I turned back to the Jaguar. "He's dying," Trébone said to no one in particular. The dark circle of apes was transfixed by his heavy breathing, but they gave him space. I stepped forward and knelt.

"Oh, Jaguar," I said, laying my hand on his head. His neck was an open wound, and his black hair was slick with blood. "Jaguar," I said, putting my face to his. My nose was tickled by the soft hair of his ears.

There was a gurgle in his throat. The apes around me leaned in closer. The Jaguar's eyes were as narrow as slits and stared ahead of him, unfocused.

"Marlin," he managed in a soft wet voice.

"My friend," I said, stroking his head. Tears streamed down my dirty face. I tasted bitter dust in my mouth.

The slit of his eye grew narrower, but I saw the pupil swing around to me. When he saw I was there, he exhaled.

With great labor he drew another breath. I felt the tremor in his chest as he tried desperately to take in air.

"Use your gift," he said. His face relaxed. Clear fluid drained from his mouth and formed a small lake across the dirt of the pit.

"Jaguar," I moaned, collapsing over him. My tears mingled with his blood and my face was wet. It had been for nothing.

Great waves of pain whipped up through my chest and threw wails from my mouth. My eyes and my face squeezed a torrent through their tiny spaces.

I lay over him. How could I use my gift now? It had caused all this. The zoo was destroyed, the animals endangered, the Jaguar killed. My father would snatch me up again and take me back to the world where I couldn't speak, where I had no friends. And the Jaguar was dead.

The pain was unbearable. It pressed through my every pore. My right palm seared and throbbed. I cried out and cradled it to my chest. The new, fresh skin writhed and shuddered and crimped. It was horrific to see. The skin bounced and pulled away from my skeleton like it wanted to escape.

Use your gift, the Jaguar had said. He had given me the gift of animal speech, but that first night when I cut my hand, wasn't there another?

The apes were creeping closer now, crowding over the Jaguar's body, and I rose up and shoved them back. "Marlin!" Trébone called as I pushed him away.

"Back!" I screamed, raising my right hand in the air. I pressed my palm to the Jaguar's neck. It came down on the wound with a wet smack, and I felt the skin tear away from me. My blood changed currents within my body, draining away from my legs and my head, all rushing toward the palm of my hand.

I felt myself falling. My vision went blurry, and then all was black.

35.

The first thing I felt was human hands gently caressing my face.

Then, sounds. A low voice moaned, "My boy, my boy, my boy, my boy, oh my boy . . ."

Then I saw chapped lips coming down over my eyes. Mustache hair tickled me as I was kissed again and again on the head.

And then the pain.

I coughed up thick black tar. My veins felt like they'd caved in. Each breath sent spikes all through my body. I tried to keep them short, but I was desperate for air. And so thirsty.

"My boy, my boy, my boy," Father droned on above me.

I managed to raise my head and look around me. Behind Father I could see that we were surrounded by apes. Trébone stood chief among them, looking at me in awe. All the apes did. My vision was still foggy, and I blinked my eyes to clear it.

The Jaguar was there, standing next to Trébone.

Blood rushed back into my body, and I tried to sit up. My father was on top of me, weighing me down.

"L—lll—leave me!" I said.

"I won't leave you, my boy. I promise," Father answered, mistaking my meaning. I summoned what strength I had and pushed him away from me. I saw the palm of my right hand. It was burned black like it been in a fire, and a horrible scar crossed where I'd cut myself that first night.

Father sat back into the dirt and I leaped up, racing toward the Jaguar.

"Marlin!" he purred happily, and raised up his head. I knelt before him.

"You're alive."

The wound had disappeared from his neck. In its place was hairless, smooth skin. He laughed heartily and licked my face.

"What do we do with him?" asked Trébone uncertainly. The circle of apes had closed in on my father, waiting for orders.

I spun to them. "You're not to hurt that man!" I said, feeling power in my lungs. Trébone looked to the Jaguar, who made no objection. "He is my father," I said. "And if you hurt

him, men from the city will follow us into the jungle. They will try to kill us in revenge."

The Jaguar turned to me quizzically.

I smiled at him and considered the circle of animals sur-rounding us. "I'll be coming with you."

The Jaguar purred and showed his teeth. "Are you our protector now?" he asked, half joking.

At my feet, Father was breathing heavily. The Jungle Look was in his eyes.

I lowered myself to help him sit up. He glanced nervously behind me at the Jaguar.

"Marlin?" he asked, shaking. "What are you?"

I put a hand on his wrinkled cheek and wiped mud from his lips with my thumb. Out of my front pocket I took the shriveled Paw that I'd once prized so much. Looking at it now, I saw it was only the hand of a creature he'd killed. I pressed it into his palm and closed his fingers round it.

"I'm m-mm-more than I knew," I stammered. "M-mm-more than I eh-eh-ever imagined."

 229

36.

The fire was smoldering down in the trees, and the Jaguar and I led a party of animals away from the peak of the pyramid.

A foghorn sounded, and through the clearing smoke I could see the *Saint of the Animals* entering port.

The Jaguar had told me to grab hold of his fur, and he leaped from stone to stone with me on his back. We descended the steps of the Golden Path at breakneck speed. The apes were opening all the cages, and the animals of the zoo stampeded behind us.

We found Kenji up in a tree, and the Jaguar scaled the trunk as though it were nothing. I picked her off a branch, and the three of us went crashing to the ground.

"What's happening?" she shouted.

"We're going home, Kenji," I assured her.

Animals from all over the zoo were with us. We even

took care to crack open the Snake House door for Dead Eyes. We led them through the Grand Gate in waves while the guests watched from the safety of the Great Hall.

Past the clearing and the stupefied sailors docking the *Saint of the Animals*, we ushered them all into the forest and watched as they disappeared by the dozen: elephants, tapirs, snakes, lizards, apes, sloths, armadillos, dogs, boars, all absorbed into the shaking trees.

When there were none left but Kenji and the Jaguar, I pointed across the clearing to the yellow wall of the resort and asked if we could scale it.

"Hold tight," the Jaguar said. I clung to his back and Kenji clung to mine. He bounded forward and leaped onto the wall, digging his claws into the cracks between the bricks. I hung precariously from his hair. Kenji screamed, but I just laughed.

Once we reached the top of the wall, we watched. The Zoo at the Edge of the World was no longer there. The dying embers in the trees illuminated the pathways and half-burned buildings. But there were no animals in the cages along the path, no workers making their rounds. It was no longer a resort. Everything had burned away. The ancient temple still stood, littered with a few modern buildings that would soon be claimed by the jungle.

The guests had left the Great Hall and were bravely making their way through the Grand Gate toward the *Saint of the Animals*. They took nothing with them. I peered into the crowd and spotted Olivia with her parents. She was far away and looked small as a cricket. Still, I watched her stop and look in my direction.

Did she see me? I couldn't tell. She didn't wave or even stop for long. It made me feel that I hadn't fulfilled my promise. I'd told her she'd see me again. My heart pulled me toward her for a moment, but I ignored it.

She boarded the boat, and I wondered if we'd ever again be close enough to touch.

Then Father came into view. He limped his way to the dock, refusing the aid of a sailor. Everyone gave him a wide berth.

Ronan Rackham came to the jungle when he was fourteen and built himself an empire. Now, forty-six years later, he was leaving again, keeping only what he'd brought with him.

Nothing.

What would become of this place without him? Georgetown grew every day, and men like the duke had eyes for jungle riches.

Father never thought he had done anything wrong. He'd desecrated a temple to make use of it. He'd captured animals to care for them. He'd ordered Nathtam killed to keep what he had.

Father did love the jungle, and he wanted to be its protector. I couldn't fault him for that. But I'd learned something he never knew.

You cannot be a conqueror *and* a protector. You cannot

preserve the jungle from men like the duke while being a man like him.

Father trudged up the gangplank and into the ship without glancing over his shoulder.

His life's work lay behind him in ruins, and he never looked back. Was that the Rackham way?

I decided to try it myself. I gave the Jaguar a pat and smiled at Kenji. Heaving myself onto his back, I gripped the Jaguar's fur as he gracefully descended the wall, stone by stone. Kenji bounced happily on my shoulder, and when we touched down on the clearing outside the wall, she pointed and cried, "The jungle, Master Marlin, the jungle!"

The line of trees was in front of us. The sounds of birds and monkeys formed a symphony. Beneath me, the Jaguar purred, and I squeezed him with my legs.

Then—as quickly as Ronan Rackham had walked out of the jungle, perhaps never to return—his son Marlin, along with a tamarin monkey named Kenji and a strange old black jaguar called just that, walked happily into it.

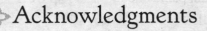

Acknowledgments

My greatest thanks to Nick and Matt Lang, who talked out this idea with me one late night in our college apartment nearly eight years ago, and in many more apartments since. Whenever people ask me for writing advice, I always tell them, "Find friends who write." These guys are some of the best friends a writer can get.

My editor, Jordan Brown, is one of the smartest people I've met in this business, and his thoughtful edits pushed this book so much further than I ever could have on my own. If you don't believe me, write in and I'll send you some early drafts.

I'm so grateful to my agent, Erica Rand Silverman, and all the good people at Sterling Lord Literistic for keeping me going.

And, of course, I'm forever indebted to every member of Team Starkid for working with me, supporting me, and being my buddies.

My mom gave me my love of animals, and in return, I give this book to her. I hope she'll share it with every member of my human and animal family: Dad, Alyssa, Jade, Bowser, Willow, Megan, and Annie. I love you all.

This is my second book. If you'd like to let me know what you think, please email me at EKGwrites@gmail.com.